Rag Doll

by

Joe Cosentino

A Jana Lane Mystery

This is a work of fiction. Names, characters, places, and incidents are either the product of the author's imagination or are used fictitiously, and any resemblance to actual persons living or dead, business establishments, events, or locales, is entirely coincidental.

Rag Doll

Cover Art by *Debbie Taylor*

The Wild Rose Press, Inc.
PO Box 708
Adams Basin, NY 14410-0708
Visit us at www.thewildrosepress.com

Publishing History
First Vintage Rose Edition, 2016
Print ISBN 978-1-5092-1000-8
Digital ISBN 978-1-5092-1001-5

A Jana Lane Mystery
Published in the United States of America

Dedication

To Fred for everything over all these years,
to Melanie and the staff at The Wild Rose Press,
to my parents, who let me read mystery novels as a kid,
to my sister and my niece, who are my greatest fans,
to everyone who loved *Paper Doll, Porcelain Doll,*
Satin Doll, and *China Doll*
and begged for another Jana Lane mystery,
and finally to the ex-child star in each of us.

Chapter 1

1985

Jana Lane, America's most famous ex-child star, ran down the sterile white hallway. Her captor's footsteps grew closer. Jana's heart pounded in her throat, and sweat dripped down her back as she opened the heavy door and entered the room marked "Private." It was full of dark shadows.

"Ahhhhh!"

"What is it, babe?"

Jana rested her quivering back on the gold circular headboard and stared up at the ruby-red satin canopy until she caught her breath. "I had another dream."

Brian sat up next to her and wrapped his muscular arm around her shoulder. Jana took in her husband's woodsy scent as he asked, "Did the dream take place in a hospital?"

I thought you were an architect, not a psychic. "How did you know?"

He ran a strong hand through his thick chestnut-colored hair. "I know you." Kissing her cheek and nose, he added, "And I know the pattern."

"What pattern?" She threw off the silver satin sheet, got out of bed, walked past the island fireplace and floor-length oval mirror, and stood under a skylight.

His hazel gaze pierced into her. "Simon gets you an acting job. You agree to do it—without talking to me first. You have nightmares about it. Your nightmares turn to reality. You get attacked, and just in the nick of time you turn the tables on the murderer."

"You think you're so smart." She stepped into her walk-in closet, discarded the sweat-soaked silver satin nightgown, and changed into a periwinkle-blue silk nightie.

"I *am* smart. That's why I've decided you are *not* doing that television show."

Jana sat at her pink velvet-trimmed vanity. Looking in the mirror, she brushed her long strawberry-blonde locks. "*You've* decided that, have you?"

"Yes, I have. And it's for your own good, and the good of our family."

She brushed so hard her scalp burned. "I'm glad you know what's for my own good."

"*Somebody* has to."

Jana gazed into the mirror at the two watery pools of crystal-blue. "Brian, I have acted since I was five years old. It's what I do. It's what I love."

"You were America's most famous child star. As an adult, you won an Oscar and a Tony Award. When is it over?"

She threw her brush at him. "Hopefully not at forty-two years old."

"Then *when*?"

Jana rose and stood at her balcony window. She watched the cobalt sky slowly transform into an orb of gold surrounded by rays of magenta, violet, and pumpkin. "I'll stop when the offers stop." She couldn't face the reality. "Actors are able to go on well into their senior years. It's a different story for an actress. I want to work while I'm still wanted."

"*I* want you."

And I love you for that. She rejoined him on the bed. "The years that I stopped working left me hollow inside. Getting back has brought me strength, resilience, and even joy."

"Not to mention nearly getting yourself and our son murdered."

"*And* not to mention helping other people—and helping the police catch murderers."

Brian headed for the bathroom, scratching his abdominal muscles. "You're not doing the series."

"All right. Then you're not going to Florida to design the new malls."

He laughed. "It's my job, babe. It's what I trained to do. What I *love* to do."

She smiled. "Exactly." *Here it comes.* Following him into the bathroom, she added, "And B.J. is playing my son."

Brian turned on the gold falcon faucets of the glass-enclosed shower. "He's four years old."

"And he had the time of his life acting in the play with me last summer."

Brian dropped his shorts and flung off his T-shirt. She couldn't help staring at him. *How come I need to work-out over an hour a day to keep the cellulite at bay, and you go to the gym twice a week and look like a Greek god?*

Clearly enjoying her stare, he grinned. "You want to join me?"

"I thought we were having an argument."

"I surrender. We can argue for days, but it won't

get me anywhere, except to my gastroenterologist—and to sleeping in the den. Like it or not, Jana Lane, actress and amateur sleuth rides again."

"I like the way you think, Mr. Otley." She giggled. "And the way you look."

"And I like everything about you, Mrs. Otley." He wrapped his strong arms around her and pulled her inside the shower stall.

"Brian, my nightie!"

"No problem. It won't be on for long."

The warm water droplets surrounded them, and steam fogged the glass. Jana massaged the muscles along her husband's V-shaped back, and he cupped her bottom. Then they shared a long, sensuous kiss that led to an even longer lovemaking session.

****

Later that morning, Jana, Brian, and B.J. ate three-berry buckwheat pancakes at the breakfast nook between the glass wall and the stone fireplace in the kitchen. Theresa, their elderly maid, sat in her uniform at one of the two islands and stared at the portable television set on the marble countertop in front of her. With Devon, thirteen, and Ed, nine, spending the summer with their cousins in Washington, DC, the house seemed something close to quiet.

"Great breakfast, Theresa," Brian said with a tongue that matched his blue suit.

Theresa continued to stare at the television screen. "Emily made this breakfast yesterday on my soap opera."

Thank goodness for commercials. Otherwise we'd all go hungry, and the house would be a total mess.

Looking adorable in his red, white, and blue striped

shirt and matching shorts, their youngest son said, "B.J. goes on TV!"

"You know about that, huh?" Brian picked up his napkin and wiped a streak of blue off his son's chin.

B.J. jumped up and down in his swivel chair like a kangaroo on a trampoline and said to his clown rag doll, "Mommy and B.J. have a show!"

Jana wiped a stain off her peach satin robe. "Soon my son and I will be arguing over top billing."

"Clownie doesn't want you to go, Daddy."

Jana held back the tears. "Daddy has to work in Florida, B.J. But he'll be home soon." *I hope.* "Are you meeting Adam in Tampa?" Jana asked Brian before finishing her orange juice.

Brian nodded. "I design them, and Adam builds them."

"I hope Adam doesn't miss Jackson too much."

"I'll miss *you* more."

She kissed him, then giggled at his purple lips.

When they finished their breakfast, Theresa loaded the dishwasher during a commercial break while Jana helped Brian pack for his trip. Once the taxicab in front of their five-acre estate was loaded with Brian's luggage, Jana and B.J. kissed Brian goodbye under the prism chandelier in the front hallway. Brian's face glistened with aqua, gold, and amber from the sun's rays as Jana said what her heart felt, "I don't want you to go."

"And I don't want you to do the TV series," Brian replied.

They shared a long kiss.

Jana said, "Come back soon."

"I will."

"Watch B.J. on TV!" B.J. said.

He's a Lane.

Brian kissed his son's chubby cheeks and messed his chestnut hair. Then he sat next to B.J. on the window seat. "Watch out for Mommy, okay?"

"Okay, Daddy. Kiss Clownie, too."

Brian obliged. "I'll call you and Mommy every day."

Jana replied, "I'll hold you to that."

Brian rose and held her in his arms. "You're my life, babe."

Don't go. "You're my everything."

"Be careful."

"Always."

They shared another long kiss then Brian hurried into the taxi with Jana and B.J. waving on the front stoop. Jana watched the taxi drive down the long circular driveway and pass through the white stone column entrance to the estate until the taxi and Brian disappeared.

Wiping the tears from her eyes, Jana led B.J. up the circular staircase, smothered him with hugs and kisses, settled B.J. and Clownie in B.J.'s bedroom with his alphabet boxes, and asked Theresa to keep an eye on him. Then Jana headed for the master bedroom, where she changed into a canary leotard, sweatpants, and leggings, and pulled her hair back with a scrunchie. The next stop was her home gym across the hall, where Jana exercised to Madonna's "Crazy for You," "Like a Virgin," and "Material Girl." An hour later, lying on her slant board, Jana looked at the sweaty, out of breath, middle-aged woman in the mirror and couldn't believe she was once *The Little Girl on the Ranch, The*

Pink Ballerina, and *The Girl Astronaut. Thank goodness the television screen is smaller than a movie screen.*

Jana took a bath in her circular tub and dried off with a thick white 'O' monogramed towel. Next, she put on a rose-patterned sweater, jeans, and rose jellie shoes. Sitting at her vanity, she teased and layered her still thick hair, and applied rose-colored eyeshadow, rouge, and lipstick to her smooth skin and full lips.

Then she sat on her gold-trimmed chaise and used the white French provincial phone to call Devon and Ed, who after answering more questions than a hostile witness in a murder trial, assured her they were having the time of their lives swimming, diving, and boating on the lake in Washington, DC. Catching up with her best friend, Congressman Jackson Mitchell, also put her mind at ease about the safety of her two oldest children.

The doorbell rang. Jana kissed the phone and hurried down the spiral staircase with B.J. After depositing him in the playroom, Jana opened the front door to a young woman about her height, five feet two inches. "You must be Mildred O'Rourke."

"Please, call me Missy, Mrs. Otley." She blushed. "Or is it Miss Lane?"

"It's Jana. Please come in, Missy."

As they passed the playroom, B.J. ran toward the visitor. "I'm B.J."

"Hello, B.J. I'm Missy."

He held his rag doll inches away from her face. "This is Clownie."

"Hello, Clownie."

"I'm going to be on TV."

Missy gasped. "Isn't that wonderful?"

"Mommy's on the show, too."

Jana laughed. "I have the feeling B.J. will get most of the close-ups."

"I like you, Missy."

"Well, thank you, B.J. I like you, too."

Jana introduced Missy to Theresa who seemed disinterested in the young woman when Missy admitted she didn't watch television soap operas. Jana asked Theresa to watch B.J. then joined Missy in the glass-enclosed sunporch. Resting on white wicker rocking chairs with bougainvillea print seat cushions, Jana raised a sterling silver pitcher of lemonade and asked Missy, "Would you like some?"

"Thank you."

Jana poured a glass for her. Though Missy's lips looked dried and cracked, Jana noticed the girl rested the drink on the white wicker and glass end table without taking a sip. Pouring a glass for herself, Jana said, "You come highly recommended from the agency, Missy."

The girl's short dark hair and bulbous dark eyes gave her a cartoonish appearance. She fidgeted with her white blouse then pulled down the hem of her gray skirt. "I began working as a nanny right after high school. I was with the Mortons for five years."

Jana looked out at the sun caressing the Catskill Mountains and Hudson River in the distance. "Yes, the Mortons and their five children." *Even B.J. will be a breeze after taking care of five kids.* "I heard the Mortons are divorced now." *Hyde Park, New York is certainly a small town.* "Why did you leave that position?"

Missy looked down at her black bow pumps. "My

boyfriend wanted me to live with *him*."

"And now?"

"Now I'd like to live here."

Ah, the pain of first love. "That seems to be my good luck, since Mrs. Morton gave you a rave review, and B.J. seems quite taken with you."

"He's adorable. And I've never worked for a celebrity before."

Jana smiled. "You must have seen my old movies."

"No, I'm too young to have seen those."

Thanks.

"And I'm embarrassed to admit I never saw *His Obsession* and *Madam Senator*. And I don't get into New York City to see plays."

Jana took a sip of lemonade. "It's not a requirement of the job to see my work."

"But I did see you...on Sundays at Reverend Heather's church. It's a terrific place." Missy's young face hardened. "Not all churches are."

"I agree."

"I generally sit in the back toward the right...by myself."

"My husband doesn't go with *me* either."

Missy sat back on the cushion. "Matty and I aren't together any longer."

"I see."

Missy sighed. "No, I don't think you do."

Clearly she wants to tell me. "What is it, Missy?"

Missy took in a deep breath. "When I first met him, Matty was going to college to become a high school biology teacher. But he got involved with a bad crowd. He started drinking then smoking pot then...taking harder drugs. He found a church that helped him break the habit. I was glad, until he invited me to go to church with him one Sunday. It wasn't a liberal church like Reverend Heather's. The minister's sermons quoted the Bible about how a woman committed the first sin, must be subservient to her husband, and should be stoned to death if she tries to get a divorce…or marries when not a virgin." A tear brimmed her eye.

"Missy, you don't need to—"

"Before you decide whether or not to hire me, I'd like you to know the truth." Missy sighed. "Since Matty and I had…been together, he told me I was…unclean. And that God wouldn't forgive me unless I joined Reverend Fowler's church, repented, and accepted my *true* role as a woman."

Meaning a second-class citizen. "Missy, do you know a sin mentioned twenty-five times in the Bible?"

Missy shook her head.

"Being left-handed. That's why, like Reverend Heather, I believe the Bible is for inspiration not law."

Missy nodded. "I was glad that Matty found his way out of addiction, and I loved him with all my heart. But I couldn't go to a place like that." Missy wiped the tear from her eye. "So after two years together, Matty left me, and he went on a missionary trip to Uganda. And he took my money with him." Missy leaned forward in her chair. "I talked to Reverend Heather. I forgave Matty. I also wrote a letter to my parents in Wisconsin. They moved there for my father's job. I asked them to forgive me, too, and they told me they did."

"Good. Now there's only one person left to forgive you."

"Who?"

"You. It's time to forgive yourself."

Missy nodded. "Jana, I'll understand if you don't want to hire me."

Jana slid to the edge of her seat. "Missy, do you know the best thing about the past?"

The girl shook her head from side to side.

"It's the *past*. So let it go. Tomorrow is a new day. The first day you'll be working for me."

Missy smiled. "You really are a nice lady, Jana." She walked around the white wicker swing to the doorway.

Jana joined her and rested a hand on Missy's shoulder. "I look forward to seeing you at seven-thirty in the morning with your luggage in hand. I'll need you with B.J. here at home, and on the set when we shoot our television show at the old, closed TB hospital in town.

"Thank you, Jana. I'll do my best."

"That's all *anyone* asks."

Jana had no sooner gone over Missy's duties and said goodbye to the girl when Jana's next visitor appeared at her large double doors. Once they were seated in the music room on the Prussian blue couch, Jana's agent adjusted the scarlet scarf over his chartreuse jumpsuit. "Here we go again, baby doll."

Having left B.J. with Theresa—and Theresa's soap opera—Jana took in the little man who was a father figure to her. "How are you, Simon?" She sipped apple cinnamon herbal tea from a china cup.

Simon Huckby, somewhere between sixty and dinosaur, squeezed her hand. "I'm always better when I see you, baby girl." He stared at the Jana Lane movie posters on the twilight blue wall in front of him. "You were the first six-year-old to star in a movie—*Daddy's Girl. The Adorable Orphan* made more money than *Gone with the Wind.* British scientists recently discovered a hole in the Earth's ozone layer, but you did it first in *The Girl Detective.* Christa McAuliffe the schoolteacher rode into space this year in the Space Shuttle Challenger, but you did it before her in *Girl Astronaut. The Littlest Farmer* and *Little Girl on the Ranch* caused people to leave cities in droves and head for the farmlands. *The Tiny Eskimo* and *Hawaiian Holiday* made Alaska and Hawaii the top travel destinations in the world. After *The Sweet Candy Striper* was released, girls lined up for blocks in front of hospitals begging to change bedpans."

"I know my ancient history, Simon."

A tear stained his eye. "And do you know that you mean more to me than anyone else in this world?"

She kissed the bald man's sunken cheek. "I know, Simon."

"Good." He reached for an almond cookie on a silver tray resting on the Louis XIV end table. "Now let's talk about your upcoming project, baby doll."

And about your ten percent.

The emaciated man bit into the cookie then adjusted his girdle, a familiar gesture for Jana. "I negotiated a terrific deal with the reps from the television network and Nevgere Productions."

"I've never heard of them."

"New production companies pop up in the night like the bed sheets of teenage boys." Simon ran a moistened finger over an eyebrow. "In negotiations I *casually* mentioned your Academy Award nomination for *His Obsession* and win for *Madame Senator.* And your Tony Award for *China Doll*." He rubbed his hands together like a pool shark after a big win. "And they bit the bullet big time. Ten episodes, including the pilot, guaranteed sight unseen. Your name above the title. Producer credit. Creative control. A six-figure salary— per episode. Profit sharing—including distribution, reruns, foreign markets, video, games, and toys. And all the episodes will be shot right here in the good old Hudson Valley, New York, the home of Jana Lane. Not to mention you'll be off on Sundays to go to your church with the lesbian minister. Keeping it all in the family, B.J. gets special 'introducing' credit for his role as your son on the show, and Cornelius wrote the theme song!"

Jana smiled at the thought of Simon's life partner; rail thin at seven feet tall in his suspenders and bowtie.

Simon hummed a catchy tune. "You'll love the theme song. I can't get it out of my head." He smiled. "And I can't get Cornelius out of my heart." Simon wiped his eyes with his cloth napkin. "I love him so dearly."

And you'll love the ten percent of the music royalties. "I'm surprised you didn't hire out Theresa to clean the closed hospital before the shoot."

"Don't tempt me."

"Simon this all sounds wonderful, but—"

"You're having nightmares about being in a hospital."

She choked on her tea. "How did you know?"

"You always have nightmares before a new project. And they usually come true." He grasped another cookie. "Baby doll, murder follows you around like a televangelist follows tax-exempt donations."

Simon reached for more cookies as if popcorn at the movie theatre. "What does Brendan say about your latest dreams?"

She frowned. "His name is Brian, and you know it."

Simon raised his small palms to the turquoise wall sconces. "How am I supposed to remember a commoner's name?"

"Brian is not a commoner."

"He's not in show business. He's a commoner." He folded his thin arms over his narrow chest. "I always said you should marry someone in the business." Simon looked from side to side like a secret agent with a stiff neck. "Where is he anyway?"

"Brian left for Tampa on business."

"Thank goodness."

"Simon!"

"We don't need any negative energy. Shooting starts tomorrow."

"You said shooting starts next week."

Simon nodded like a mahjong player with a winning tile. "With *Murder She Wrote* and *Miami Vice* such big hits, the network wants the pilot ASAP. And why wouldn't they? *The Detective's Wife* stars my baby girl! As you know, you play the wife of a detective who solves crimes under her husband's nose. Just like my baby doll solves mysteries in real life." He swallowed some tea. "Do you know your lines?"

"Of course. But if I have creative control, how come I haven't met anyone on the creative team?"

He waved her away like a gnat at a picnic. "I took care of all that for you, baby doll." He inhaled more cookies.

"Can you at least tell me the name of my director and co-stars?"

Simon looked at the empty cookie tray and said like Oliver Twist, "May I have another cookie first?"

Jana summoned Theresa who brought more cookies with B.J. hurrying behind her.

"Here's my little star!" Simon scooped B.J. up into his short arms.

"Mama's agent!" B.J. nuzzled his cheek into Simon's neck then played with Simon's lime waist pouch.

"I'm *your* agent, too!"

"Simon!" B.J. said merrily.

"That's right, B.J. And I am going to make you a big star—like I did for your mother."

Don't break out into a chorus of "Everything's Coming Up Roses," Simon.

"This is Clownie." B.J. presented his rag doll to Simon.

Simon examined the doll. "I don't represent clowns."

Since Theresa's soap opera commercial break was over, Jana gave B.J. a big hug then Theresa and B.J. left for the kitchen.

Simon took a wrinkled paper and old spectacles out of his waist pouch and read, "Herm Fenton is directing."

"I know the name."

"He's coming off a hit series. We're lucky to have him." Simon glanced down again at his paper. "Christa Bianca is the first episode's guest star."

Jana rubbed her forehead. "Where have I heard that name?"

Simon clutched at his emaciated chest. "Probably on every entertainment television show lately." He added like a gossip columnist on a sugar high, "Christa Bianca is the young, gorgeous ingénue who made a huge splash—literally—in the indie feature about the female autistic diver. But she isn't."

"Isn't autistic or a diver?"

"Either. Christa and her manager husband, Andrew, told her rags to riches story to Barbara Walters. They came from a little mountain town, Renovo, PA. When the forest was stripped by natural disaster, the little lumber town went bust. Christa's father died from lung cancer and probably starvation, and her mother followed soon after from a broken heart. In her senior year at high school, her sweetheart, Andrew, convinced her to enter the Miss Flaming Foliage Pageant at the Flaming Foliage Festival. Luckily for Christa, Stu Silverman happened to be in Philly to meet with a producer, and Stu caught Christa's tearful pageant acceptance speech on local television from his hotel room. As they say, a star was born. And Stu has been her agent ever since." He licked his lips like a dog at a weenie roast. "I admire loyalty in a client."

Down boy, you've been my agent since I was six.

"Christa always admired her uncle, the character actor, Nicholas Hartford. She followed in his footsteps to Hollywood. However, he took a detour—to the bottle. By the time he supposedly dried out, his career was dried out, too. She helped him out by getting Nick a juicy role in the episode."

"It seems like Christa has a strong sense of roots."

"And a strong agent." Simon shuddered. "I hate

those. Stu got Christa top guest star billing. She plays the young nurse on the show who discovers the hospital is selling organs for profit. As you know, this puts her in peril, and she confides in you. As an amateur sleuth, you snoop around the hospital and figure out the culprit is the hospital administrator, played by Nicholas Hartford with second guest star billing. This of course puts your life in danger, culminating in a big showdown with you and Christa's Uncle Nick, where you save yourself and your son, B.J., from the murderer just as your husband, the detective, finally arrives clueless on the scene."

"I know the plot, Simon. Tell me about the rest of the cast?"

Simon scanned his paper. "Let's see. Bit players. It says there are two couples in real life: Hyo Tsu and Aisha Sanchez play an orderly and intern respectively. Alaster Temple and Siobhan MacAuley play a young doctor and nurse. And Karen Evans is Nicholas' first victim, the nurse who tries to blackmail him. In real life, Karen is the wife of the actor playing your husband on the series."

Jana smelled a Hollywood rat. "Simon, you haven't told me the name of the actor who plays my husband."

"Haven't I?" Simon looked like a kid caught emptying the cookie jar—literally. "He's a new client of mine. Someone who will make a good husband for you—on screen and off."

Jana offered Simon a no nonsense look. "Who is it, Simon?"

A ruggedly handsome man entered the room. "Theresa let me in. I brought lunch: seared tuna, baby greens, beets, asparagus, goat cheese, and pistachio nuts with an orange vinaigrette. This room is too fancy. Let's eat in your sunroom."

Jana's jaw dropped and her mouth salivated at the sight of ex-professional quarterback, Detective Christopher Bove from Washington, DC.

The three of them ate lunch on the sunporch. Then Cornelius arrived on his motorcycle to drive Simon home. Jana settled B.J. in his bedroom for a nap, and Jana and Bove walked past Theresa watching her soap opera in the kitchen and went out the rear French doors. As they passed the hot tub, heart-shaped pool, and cabana, Jana took in the tall, extremely muscular man with a perfectly square jaw. "Thanks for lunch. As always it was delicious. How is your parents' restaurant?"

Dressed in his usual black leather jacket, white dress shirt, and black chino slacks, Bove's emerald eyes glistened in the afternoon sun. "It still has the best food in DC."

"Is your brother still the chef there?"

He ran a thick hand through his jet-black hair and his bicep nearly burst through his jacket. "Don't do it, Jana."

"I didn't mention Allison."

"I knew it."

"Why are you still upset over Allison leaving you at the altar for your brother?"

"Gee, I don't know. Maybe I thought I'd spend the rest of my life with the woman I loved, who accepted my wedding proposal, and planned a wedding with me."

"When I last saw you in Washington, DC, you were engaged to a senator."

"Did you have to bring that up?"

Jana stopped at the entrance to her garden. "*She* dumped you, *too*?"

He nodded. "She was unhappy."

And clearly insane.

They continued walking past the multi-colored flowers over the small bridge with the mountains in the distance.

"Unhappy women seem to follow you around, Bove."

"Like murder follows *you*."

She smiled. "We were a good team in DC."

"*The Adorable Orphan* saved the day."

"And now you're an actor?"

"I had some offers after I gave up football. I didn't take them seriously. I wanted to be a detective."

"And you were a good one."

"Thanks to a lot of help from *The Girl Detective*."

Jana rested against the entrance post to her riding stable. "I was also *The Jungle Girl*. So unless you want me to chase you up that tree, come clean, Bove."

He leaned his mountainous back against the post next to her. Their shoulders touched, and Jana's knees quivered. "When we all met up in DC, Simon asked me if I wanted to get into show business—with him as my agent."

"You never told me."

"I didn't think much about it, until I married an actress, Karen. I mentioned it to her, and she pushed me to call Simon and accept."

"How come Karen didn't leave you at the altar?"

"We got married at the justice of the peace."

"Good move."

"Karen's stage name is Karen Evans. Simon made a package deal for the show with you, me, B.J., and Karen. She plays Nurse One. She auditioned for the larger role of the main nurse, but she didn't get it."

"Christa Bianca's role?"

"Don't say that name."

"Were you engaged to Christa Bianca, *too*?"

"Very funny." He continued walking on the grass, and she followed. "Karen's a bit jealous of Christa. After graduating from college as a theater major, Karen's done some commercials, a few plays, and lately some bit roles on TV. She's frustrated that larger roles haven't come along. She's thirty years old, which is middle age if you're not a star."

It's middle age if you're a star, too. Hence my move from movies to television. Jana thought of her nephew's quest for instant stardom. "It takes time to find success in show business."

"What were you, like six when you starred in your first movie?"

"I am certainly not the norm."

"That's for sure."

She pushed him away, and he ran after her. "How did you and Karen meet?"

"I'm not telling you."

"I'm not giving up. Are you going to tackle me like in your glory days, Bove?"

"No way. After those fight scenes in your movies, you'd wipe the grass with me."

She picked up a blade of grass and tickled his neck. "Don't make me torture you, Bove. I was *The Pirate Princess*, remember?"

"All right. Promise you won't laugh."

"Of course. I'm not a child, Bove."

"Karen was Allison's maid of honor."

Jana burst out laughing.

Bove walked away.

She ran and caught up to him. "Come on, Bove. It's funny."

"To *you*."

"It should be to you, too. You ended up with the right woman. And you were offered the detective role on my show. All's well in TV land."

"Not exactly. Karen and I are separated."

She laughed again. "I'm sorry."

"No you're not. *I'm* sorry since Karen and I are staying at the hotel with the rest of the cast and crew."

Jana looked at the guest cottage in the distance.

"My guest cottage is available."

His face lit up. "You mean it?"

She nodded.

"Will Brian mind?"

"He's away in Tampa on business."

"He sure travels a lot."

"Do you want to stay in the guest cottage or not?"

"I'll move in tonight."

Looking down at her wedding ring, Jana said, "Bove, if you and Karen are separated, why did you take the TV role?"

He rested his strong hands on her shoulders and his pectoral muscles nearly ripped his shirt. "You know why I took it." His eyes bore into hers.

Jana took in his pine scent, handsome face, and incredible physique. Stopping herself from wrapping her arms around him, she continued walking to the guest cottage. "You know nothing can happen between us."

"You play my wife on the show!"

"You know what I mean. Speaking of the show, have you ever acted before?"

"Only in interrogations as a detective, and when I was interviewed as a football player."

"There's a lot to know about acting in front of the camera."

"You'll help me." He walked to the door of the guest cottage.

She was at his heels like a cat following a slipper. "You need to learn acting techniques like sense memory, emotional recall, listening and reacting, being in the moment, using your imagination, observation. And the camera angles help determine what you can do with your eyes, your face, and your body."

He laughed.

"What is it?"

"I've been taking acting lessons for months. Simon arranged them."

She slapped his shoulder playfully. "We'll see how much you've learned tomorrow."

"I hope I can hold a candle to the famous Jana Lane." As Jana opened the door for him, Bove added, "And I hope nobody gets killed before the first take."

Jana felt the blood drain from her face. "Bove, I've been having dreams about being chased at the hospital."

His face softened. "Then I'm glad I'm here."

"Me, too."

Chapter 2

Jana Lane opened the door and entered the dark room. Hearing footsteps from the hallway behind her, she followed the light escaping from under the closed door and hid behind the desk. Her throat tightened as the door opened.

The next morning, Jana rose early, shook off her nightmare, exercised in her gym, bathed, and put on a cranberry collar dress with matching shoes and earrings. Since she was headed for a shoot, she didn't bother styling her hair or applying makeup. Instead she sat on her chaise and reviewed her lines in the script. When she heard B.J. call, she hurried to his room and smothered her baby with kisses and hugs. By the time Jana washed and dressed him, Missy arrived looking pretty in an apricot blouse and jeans. With Missy unpacking in her new bedroom down the hall, Jana made a quick phone call to the three men in her family, and let B.J. say hello. Once she was satisfied they were safe and sound, and in the throes of business meetings (Brian), and boating and fishing (Devon and Ed), Jana and her entourage wished Theresa a romantic day on her soap operas and drove in a car sent from Nevgere Productions the short distance to the abandoned hospital in town.

Upon entering the hospital, after signing an autograph for the security guard, Jana was directed to a room set up with chairs and mirrors as a makeup station. A thirtyish woman with short blonde hair and big blue eyes, wearing jeans and a T-shirt, teased Jana's hair into layers around her face then applied her makeup. "You're my first celebrity, Miss Lane."

Jana said carefully without ruining her makeup, "Please call me, Jana. What's your name?"

"Cindi."

Jana looked in the mirror at the twilight-blue mascara and cherry-red rouge on her face. "You're a good makeup artist, Cindi."

Cindi glowed like an orb. "I have a little shop in town. I was thrilled when I got hired for this gig."

"I'm thrilled to have you."

Jana stepped off the chair, and B.J. took her place.

"And who do we have here?" Cindi asked, clearly already under B.J.'s spell.

"I'm B.J. She's Missy. And this is Clownie."

"It's my pleasure to take care of you, B.J."

"My pleasure, too!" B.J. giggled as Cindi applied a thin coating of base to his face.

"All done. Thanks, B.J."

"What about Clownie?"

Cindi took a clean brush and moved it around the rag doll's face. "How's that?"

"Great!"

Jana mouthed a 'thank you' to Cindi. Then Jana, B.J., and Missy were directed to an old x-ray room serving as the wardrobe station. Jana was fitted into a white high-necked sweater, slacks, and sandals, and B.J. was outfitted in a red and blue play shirt, slacks, and sneakers.

A young woman with a long face and longer

walkie-talkie hanging off the belt loop of her jeans directed them to their dressing rooms. Once they had changed, the woman led them to a reception area with chocolate-colored sofas and easy chairs in various clusters around the room. People milled around the catering table at the rear, filling their plates with various breakfast items. "What can I get you for breakfast?"

Jana offered the young woman a warm smile. "You don't have to serve me."

The woman hurried off, no doubt to accomplish her next menial task.

At the food table, Jana spooned a plate of fruit for herself and a bowl of oatmeal for B.J. Missy helped herself to eggs and juice. Once seated on a sofa, Jana placed a cloth napkin under her collar and another on her lap, a habit from years of not wanting to raise the ire of the wardrobe staff by spilling food on her clothing.

"Oh my goodness. Jana Lane!"

Jana rested her plate on the end table, rose, and offered her hand. "Hi. I'm Jana."

"Please don't get up, Miss Lane."

Jana gazed at the young woman's shiny onyx hair and eyes, peaches and cream complexion, petite striking figure, and perfectly proportioned features. Looking at the woman in her nurse's uniform, there was something homespun and accessible about her. Jana thought she must be a compassionate nurse. "Please call me Jana. Are you the nurse consultant?"

The woman offered a dimpled smile. "I'm Christa Bianca. I play one of the nurses in the episode." She shook Jana's hand. "It is such an honor to be working with you, Miss...Jana. I've seen all of your old movies so many times."

B.J. chuckled. "Mama's old."

And why did I have a third child? "Christa, it's a pleasure to meet you. This is my son B.J."

Christa kneeled next to B.J., clearly comfortable with children. "Hi, B.J., I'm Christa. Who's that?"

B.J. placed Clownie inches away from Christa's face. "Clownie. You can kiss him."

Christa obliged.

"He likes you."

"I like him, too. I had a rag doll when I was a kid. I made him out of my daddy's old T-shirt."

"My mommy bought me this one."

Christa smiled at Jana. "You have a nice mommy."

B.J. nodded. "Even though she's old."

Jana cleared her throat and finished the introductions. "Christa, this is Missy, B.J.'s nanny."

"I like Missy, too," B.J. explained.

"Hi, Christa," Missy said.

"Hello, Missy." Christa rose to her feet at the same time as Missy. "If I wasn't an actress, I think I'd be a nanny. I love kids. I raised my younger brother and sisters."

"Have you had breakfast yet?" Jana asked.

Christa nodded. "I was so nervous I got here before the building was even open. It was just a police officer in uniform, my husband, and me."

"Please sit with us."

"Thank you." Christa sat next to Jana like a handmaiden at the side of the queen. "This is all still new to me. And a bit overwhelming."

"I hear you are a terrific actress."

"I did one movie. Low budget. The good reviews

could have been a fluke."

Jana smiled. "I doubt it. Your role in this episode is quite good. You wouldn't have been cast if you weren't up to it. And I'll be here to help you in any way I can. Please count on me."

Christa blinked back a tear. "Thank you so much Miss…Jana. You're as nice as I thought you would be."

"Clownie has to go to the bathroom."

"I'll take him." Missy took B.J.'s hand and walked him out the door.

Jana and Christa sat on the sofa. A tear brimmed Christa's eye.

"What's wrong?" Jana asked.

"Sorry, I keep thinking about how proud my parents would be if they were still here."

Jana nodded. "I lost my mother to cancer when I was thirteen. I think of her every time I start shooting."

"That's about how old I was when I lost my father to lung cancer. My mother died soon after…of a broken heart. I thought it would get better as I got older. It hasn't."

Jana took her hand. "The pain never goes away. But you learn to live with it."

Christa smiled. "You really are everyone's best friend. Just like in your old movies."

Jana ate her breakfast. "How is it such a young woman has seen the old Jana Lane films?"

Christa waved her hands in front of her like a crossing guard facing a speed racer. "In Renovo, Pennsylvania, that's my hometown up in the mountains, they showed your movies at the movie theatre in town every Saturday afternoon. I never missed one. *The Cowgirl and the Bandit*, *The Littlest Farmer*, *Little Girl on the Ranch*, and *The Little Shop Girl* were my favorites, but I loved them all. When you told little Timmy you'd be friends forever then saved him from bandits, outlaws, and crooks, I cried like a fool. After my daddy and momma died, I thought about your movies. They gave me the strength to get through the rough times. I will always be grateful to you for that."

Jana squeezed her hand.

"Do you want to go over your lines?" A tall, thin, bespectacled young man wearing a dark suit a size too big for him held a script out to Christa.

Christa's face lit up like a jack-o-lantern. "I've studied those lines so long I know them better than my own name." She turned to Jana. "This is Andrew Bianca, my husband and manager. Andrew, this is Jana Lane."

Jana rose and shook his clammy hand. "Nice to meet you, Andrew."

"It's a pleasure to meet me." He blushed. "I mean, it's a pleasure to meet you."

"Andrew saw your movies with me," Christa explained.

"I liked how you wrestled that ape to save your father in *Going Ape*, and when you rode the twenty-foot wave with little Timmy on your back to rescue him from sharks in *Surf's Up*."

Christa added, "And now you save *me* from the hospital administrator in this show!"

Jana laughed. "Thank goodness I don't have to do any of those things to do it. Please join us, Andrew."

Christa took his hand. Jana noticed they seemed to relax once they were touching. "Andrew and I went through school together in Renovo."

"Christa was a better student than me." Andrew kissed her cheek.

"Studying was a nice break from my chores. We didn't even have a television set." Christa kissed Andrew's hand. "We were all poor in Renovo, but nobody was poorer than me. The kids in school called me 'Rag Doll,' like the popular song at that time."

"'Cause she was beautiful but poor," Andrew explained.

"How cruel," Jana said.

Christa giggled. "Andrew used to call me that, too."

"Until I found Christa in the cloakroom." He put his long arm around her and hugged Christa into his narrow chest.

"In the cloakroom?" Jana asked.

Christa explained, "One day after school was out, the kids called me that name, pushed me into the cloakroom, shut the light, and left. Sitting in the corner of the cloakroom, I thought about our shack at home, my hungry brother and sisters, my parents who I missed so much, and the way the other kids treated me. I started to cry, and I couldn't stop. Andrew had left his jacket, and he came back to fetch it. He saw me sitting in the closet crying, and he asked me if I was all right. For the first time in my life, somebody asked me if I was all right and really meant it."

"It broke my heart to see Christa crying like that," Andrew added.

"Andrew said he was going along with the other kids, so they wouldn't pick on him, too."

"I thought it was all in fun, but seeing Christa on that closet floor, I knew it wasn't anything near fun."

"So he apologized, helped me up and out of there, dried my cheeks with his handkerchief, and told me he'd be my protector from that day on." Christa kissed his cheek. "And he has." She rested her head on his arm. "And it was Andrew's idea that I sign up for the Flaming Foliage Festival Pageant. He even gave me the money to enter—from his job as a stock boy. I thought he was insane."

"But she was crowned queen. I knew she would be."

Christa said, "Andrew believed in me before I believed in myself. I wouldn't be here if it wasn't for my husband." A tear flowed down Christa's cheek.

Jana handed her a tissue from her purse.

"Thank you." Christa wiped her cheek. "As you can see, I wear my heart on my sleeve."

"And it's a loving heart." Andrew smiled at his wife.

"That it is." An elderly, bald man with a huge nose sat on the other side of Jana and held out a bejeweled hand. "Stu Silverman, Christa's agent."

As Jana shook Stu's wrinkled hand, Christa explained, "Stu was traveling through Renovo to Philly. He turned on the TV in his hotel room and happened to see me being interviewed after the pageant."

"And as they say, the rest is history. Christa was wonderful in the indie film. And she'll be terrific on your show."

"I don't doubt it," Jana said.

More tears flowed as Christa pointed at Stu. "This man literally saved my life. He rescued me from poverty and helped me get my brother and sisters out of Renovo and into a good boarding school. Acting and voice lessons, dental work, professional pictures, plane fare to Los Angeles, he paid for it all. I will never forget that."

"I knew a special talent when I saw it." Stu winked at Christa.

Jana noticed Bove walk into the room. Her pulse quickened at the sight of his muscles bursting out of a gold sweater and black chinos. Next to him was a hard-looking blonde woman of about thirty. Jana waved to Bove, and they joined Jana's group. "Christa, Andrew, and Stu, this is Chris Bove who plays my husband in the show."

Bove said, "Jana Lane and company, this is Karen Evans."

"Soon to be his ex-wife," Karen said.

Charming.

Ignoring Karen, Bove asked Jana, "What did you eat for breakfast?"

"Fruit," Jana replied.

"You need more than fruit. I'll be right back."

With Bove headed for the food table, Jana invited Karen to sit with them.

"Hi, I'm Christa Bianca." Looking at Karen's nurse's uniform, she added, "You must be playing a nurse, too."

Karen sneered. "I have the good fortune of playing Nurse One who gets killed on page three of the script."

Three pages too late as far as I'm concerned.

Obviously not catching Karen's sarcasm, Christa replied, "How nice. I play the nurse who uncovers that the hospital is selling organs for profit, which puts me in peril."

"I remember"—Karen added with disdain—"when

I read for the role."

Christa continued. "This is my husband and manager Andrew, and my agent Stu."

Karen said, "It must be nice to have an entourage."

Christa guffawed. "Is *that* what I have?"

"Most definitely. And I am proud to be included." Character actor Nicholas Hartford's silver hair reflected in the overhead fluorescent lighting. Though well past middle age, he looked regal and dapper in his blue pin-striped suit.

Christa rose and threw her arms around him. "Uncle Nick! It's so good to see you!"

Nick returned the hug, and introductions were made all around. As they shook hands, Jana smelled bourbon on his breath.

Sitting on an easy chair opposite them, Nick said, "When I visited Christa's parents between my film shoots, this little girl would sit on my knee and tell me, 'I want to be an actor, just like you, Uncle Nick.' Now Christa recommended me for this job, and I couldn't be more proud to work with my beautiful niece."

Christa beamed like a headlight. "When I was a girl, I couldn't wait for Uncle Nick's visits. He'd bring my brother and sisters toys and a pretty new dress for me. I'd tell him how much I wanted to be in show business like him. Secretly hoping he would take me with him when he left." Christa added, "Those dreams with you, Uncle Nick, were what kept me going after my parents passed on."

The elderly man squeezed her hand. "I'm sorry I missed the funeral. I was on a film shoot. But you and your brother and sisters were in my heart and prayers as always."

Bove returned with a plate full of quiche Lorraine, Portobello mushrooms stuffed with crabmeat and Gouda cheese, a blueberry banana walnut whole wheat muffin, and mixed greens with almond slivers and baby tomatoes. He handed Jana the plate. "Eat this."

If acting doesn't work out, being a waiter is definitely not an option for you, Bove. "Thank you."

"Yes, Jana, Bove is very attentive…until he loses interest," Karen said.

Steam nearly came out of his ears, as Bove walked away. Jana placed her overflowing plate on the end table and followed him. They met at a large window overlooking the mountains in the distance. "Is she always like that?"

Bove laughed bitterly. "So you noticed." His thick thumb rubbed against his forehead. "She wasn't like this in the beginning."

"What was she like?"

"Understanding about my last two break-ups. Interested in my past in football and as a detective." He sighed. "I realize now she was using my celebrity to try to break into show business."

"Was Allison impressed by your years as a star quarterback?"

"You had to say that name, didn't you?"

Jana ignored his sarcasm. "Have you moved into the guest cottage yet?"

He nodded. "Just before I got here."

"Have no fear, Mama is here!" Simon, wearing a fuchsia and maize jumpsuit, kissed each of their cheeks. "How are my two favorite clients?"

"We're your *only* clients, except for B.J."

Simon winked at her. "My perfect family. Mother,

33

father, and son."

"I'm married to Brian, Simon."

"A mere technicality in Hollywood." Simon grinned like the Cheshire Cat. "You two belong together."

Jana noticed four young people dressed in hospital whites sitting together in a corner of the room. She learned at a young age from her father to introduce herself to the other actors on the set. "Simon, please talk to your new client about the dangers of obsessing about his exes."

"What exes?" Simon asked like a gossip columnist.

"Karen and Allison," Jana replied with a grin.

Bove groaned. "You had to say it!"

Jana approached the four young people sitting with their heads together. A handsome Asian American man and a stunning African American woman shared a loveseat. On the loveseat opposite them sat a nice-looking Caucasian couple.

"Welcome, I'm Jana Lane."

The four of them leaped to attention as if privates meeting a general at platoon inspection.

Ah, that frozen-eyed, enamored, vacant stare so many people offer celebrities, as if we are gods and goddesses of perfection. If they only knew we are real people just like them with the same hopes, fears, and frailties.

"It's such a pleasure to meet you, Miss Lane. We loved your first movie, *His Obsession*."

My first movie. Ah, youth.

"Almost as much as we loved your second one, *Madame Senator*."

"Thank you. I'm Jana. What are your names?"

"Intern One."

"Your *real* names?"

"Oh, I'm Aisha Borel." The African American woman shook Jana's hand.

"And I'm her boyfriend, Hyo Tsu. I play Orderly Two." He shook Jana's hand.

"It's a pleasure to meet you both. And *you* are?"

A young woman with long auburn hair and green eyes shook Jana's hand. "I'm Siobhan MacAuley, Nurse Two. This is my boyfriend, Alaster Temple."

The tall, thin man with blond hair and blue eyes shook Jana's hand. He spoke with a British accent. "I'm Young Male Doctor."

"We loved *China Doll*," Aisha and Siobhan said in unison.

"Girls night out," explained Aisha.

"We can't get these guys to go to Broadway," Siobhan added.

Jana laughed. "I understand. I was happy my husband came." She looked behind her. "Have you met Chris Bove, Karen Evans, Nicholas Hartford, and Christa Bianca?"

They looked as if Jana had offered them sour milk.

"What's wrong?" Jana asked.

The foursome exchanged glances like secret agents in enemy territory.

"Please, what is it?"

Siobhan answered, "We got here early and Christa Bianca…met us, Miss Lane."

"Please, call me Jana. Was there a problem with Christa?"

Hyo started to answer, but Aisha spoke over him, "No, no problem."

Their acting believability needs work. "I'm also listed as a producer on this series. Something my agent arranged. So if you have a concern, please tell me, and I'll try to help if I can."

Again Hyo opened his mouth. This time Aisha wrapped her arm through his. "No problem. Thank you for asking, though."

"Please remember what I said."

Alaster started to speak, but Siobhan took his hand. "Thank you, Jana."

"See you on set." When Jana returned to her party, she found Simon, having eaten her breakfast plate, swapping agent stories with Christa's agent, Stu Silverman. She noticed Missy and B.J. were back from the bathroom and engrossed in a board game. Christa sat next to her uncle, lost in his story of past stardom, as she no doubt was during her childhood. Bove and Karen were in heated battle. Noticing Christa's husband sitting alone, looking like a wallflower at his first dance, Jana sat next to him. "I forget how boring waiting around on sets can be. My sister did it throughout my childhood. I give her a great deal of credit."

Andrew pushed his black glasses up the bridge of his nose, revealing large brown eyes. "Christa went through so much. She deserves this."

"And she has a supportive husband. That helps." *Not that I know anything about that.* "It looks like Christa is headed for a long and fruitful career."

He gazed at Christa with love filling his thin face. "And I'll be right beside her every step of the way."

Since Nicholas had finished his no doubt embellished story about starring in a B movie thirty years ago, Christa excused herself to go to the ladies' room.

Missy said to Jana, "I have to make a phone call. Would you mind watching B.J.?"

"Of course not." Jana excused herself and sat on an easy chair with B.J. on her lap, reading him a story about clowns, his new favorite fascination.

The assistant director, a tired-looking elderly man, shouted for quiet. Then the executive producer, a tall woman in a pants suit with shoulder pads that accentuated her already broad shoulders, introduced herself to Jana as Sybil Harrington-Burlington. Before Jana could reply, the woman stood in front of the room and read a welcome speech to everyone involved in *Jana Lane in The Detective's Wife*. The woman's gold jewelry jangled like a reindeer at Christmas as she wished everyone a good shoot.

I hope Simon is right about the solvency of Nevgere Productions.

Three men in business suits entered the room, and the executive producer scurried to their side like a squirrel in a chestnut field.

The television network executives no doubt.

Missy and Christa walked back into the room as if they had witnessed an earthquake.

Jana asked Missy, "What's wrong?"

"Nothing. I'm fine." Her face drained of color, Missy looked pleadingly at Christa then took B.J. to sit on a sofa near the window.

Jana sat next to Christa on the sofa. "What was *that* about?"

Before Christa could respond, a middle-aged, thin man with graying temples, pockmarks on his pale face, and bitten off nails, stood at the front of the room. "I'm Herm Fenton, the director. A few things. This is television, so we shoot quickly. Since the exteriors will be shot just outside the hospital, and the interiors will all be in the hospital, we're shooting in sequence. We'll rehearse and shoot on each set before each take. The A. D. is passing out a schedule. Know your lines and be ready when a P.A. calls you. That's it."

Lucky for Herm he's not a social director.

Jana noticed Karen Evans heading for Herm like a hunter spotting a blind deer. Karen elegantly extended her hand to the director. "I'm Karen Evans. I play Nurse One. The casting director called me back for Christa's role." She glared at Christa a few feet away. "But that obviously didn't work out."

"I don't have anything to do with casting." Herm scanned his script.

"I've heard such great things about you"—Karen offered a sexy, full-lipped smile—"from Joanna St. Claire."

That caught his attention.

Herm looked up at Karen for the first time. "You know Joanna, do you?"

Karen purred like a just-fed kitten. "Joanna and I were close friends when I lived in LA. She told me what a great...director you were on her last TV shoot. She said you two...worked very well together."

"She's a good actress."

Karen batted her mascara-laden lashes and blinked her baby-blue eyes. "Back in LA, people used to confuse the two of us. Do you think I resemble her?"

Herm smiled. "I can see the resemblance."

She moved closer. "Joanna and I have a lot in

common."

As Bove stood next to Jana, she could feel his anger. "Does she always do this when meeting a director?"

Bove groaned. "Sickening, isn't it?"

Jana watched Karen and Herm walk off to a corner of the room. "You sure know how to pick them, Bove."

"Speaking of picking them, I'm guessing Brian was thrilled and supportive about you doing a TV series."

Jana softened her voice. "He's worried about my nightmares."

"Did you have another dream last night?"

She nodded.

A production assistant, who didn't look much older than Jana's son Devon, led Jana to meet the officious network executives. Then he asked Jana, Bove, and B.J. to follow him. While he listened to orders squawking from his walkie-talkie, the assistant led them outside into a minivan for a short ride to a park nearby. When they got out of the minivan, Cindi met them for makeup touch-ups. Jana noticed how Cindi took extra care with Bove, resting her hand on his shoulder as she worked. Bove seemed to enjoy the attention, offering Cindi a wink when she was finished. Jana whispered to Bove, "Looks like you got special treatment."

"Stop being jealous," he replied.

"I'm not jealous."

"Yes you are."

Herm directed Jana and Bove to run after B.J. on the Kelley-green grass and push him on the swing and slide.

Standing together on the mowed lawn, Jana

explained to B.J., "Bove is your pretend dad."

B.J. threw his arms around Bove. "I like my pretend dad."

Bove's strong features softened as he returned the hug. "I like you, too, B.J."

"Roll camera! Slate! Action!"

The three actors followed Herm's direction for the scene. Jana and Bove had an easy and honest rapport. B.J. took to the camera in the same way he reveled onstage.

He's definitely a Lane.

Then Herm explained the next shot. While B.J. played in the sandbox, Jana and Bove would have a romantic moment on the bench nearby, looking out at the Hudson River wrapping its delicate fingers around the sun-kissed Bear Mountains. As the production assistant lifted the slate in front of them, Jana couldn't help wondering what her life would be like married to Bove.

You're married to Brian, remember, the love of your life, and the father of your three children?

"Roll camera! Slate! Action!"

As Jana and Bove sat on the bench, his pine scent filled her nostrils. He took her in his powerful arms and ran his thick fingers through her hair. She looked up into his eyes begging for affection. Placing her hands on his V-shaped back, their lips touched, and Jana surrendered to a long, passionate kiss.

"Cut! Check the gate then let's move to the next location!"

Jana rose on shaky legs.

"You all right?" Bove asked with a twinkle in his eyes.

She used her acting skills in a failed attempt at sounding natural. "I'm fine."

"I was hoping we'd need a second take."

Jana sounded like a business executive. "I believe we got it right the first time."

His dimple appeared. "So it seems."

B.J. ran into her arms. "I like this, Mommy. It's fun!"

It sure is, B.J.

The production assistant drove them back to the hospital. Following more squawking on the walkie-talkie, he walked them to a small room which had been transformed by the set designer into a little boy's bedroom. Again Cindi touched up Jana's, B.J.'s, and Clownie's makeup. Cindi asked Jana, "Doesn't the man playing your husband need a touch-up?"

Down girl. "Bove isn't in this scene. He's in the next one."

"Good." Cindi turned scarlet. "I mean, it's good that the scenes are moving along so well. You're a good actress."

You aren't. "Thanks, Cindi."

Once B.J. was settled under the bedcovers, Herm directed Jana to tuck B.J. into his sleigh bed and kiss him goodnight. The director liked B.J.'s suggestion for Jana to kiss and tuck in Clownie, too.

Everybody's a director.

The slate was called, and they shot the scene. Jana found little challenge in acting her love for her son. B.J. was a natural at pretending to fall asleep in bed as he often did at home.

Missy took charge of B.J. The wardrobe woman whisked Jana away to her dressing room, where Jana changed into a tangerine satin nightgown then followed another production assistant with the same squawking walkie-talkie to yet another room set up as a well-furnished master bedroom. Herm asked Jana to climb into bed next to Bove, who was already positioned under the sheet with his shirt off. Jana gasped at the sight of Bove's incredibly sculpted physique. Trying not to stare at his mountainous pectoral muscles and washboard abdominals, she lifted the sheet to hop in, happy to find Bove wearing slacks.

The king-sized bed was lit, and the boom microphone placed over them. Behind the camera in the dim light stood other cast and crew members ready to watch the scene. In the shadows, Jana could make out the figures of Christa and Andrew Bianca, Christa's uncle Nicholas Hartford, Christa's agent Stu Silverman, Karen Evans, the two young couples Hyo Tsu and Aisha Borel and Alaster Temple and Siobhan MacAuley, and of course Simon, Missy, and B.J.

Herm directed the scene, where Jana and Bove talked about his rough day at work, cuddled in bed, then Jana experienced her appendicitis attack. Jana asked the nurse consultant for the specific area and intensity of her pain for a realistic performance.

As they rehearsed the scene, Jana massaged Bove's strong shoulders then rested against his firm chest. He added an unscripted kiss, and Jana didn't balk. Jana's concerns about Bove's inexperience as an actor quickly vanished. She was thrilled to find Bove quite relaxed, in touch with his emotions, and believable in the character. However, Jana wasn't surprised to note she and Bove had incredible chemistry together. When it came time for Jana's appendicitis attack, she doubled over as if in terrible pain with tears filling her eyes. Bove leaped up with horror in his eyes and asked if she was all right.

"Stay under the sheet, Bove. Okay, let's shoot it," Herm shouted.

As the lighting crew adjusted a light and the slate was prepared, Bove leaned back on the headboard and caught his breath. "I thought you were really in pain."

"It's called acting," Jana said.

Cindi freshened their makeup, taking extra time to comb Bove's hair. Jana thought Bove looked like a puppy getting his tummy rubbed.

Herm called for, "Roll camera! Slate! Action!"

Jana and Bove did the scene. It went well, this time with Bove staying in character when Jana became ill.

When the camera, lights, and boom microphone were in place for Jana's close-up and Herm called for action, Jana and Bove did the scene again with a thin piece of gauze over the camera lens aimed at Jana.

Ah, the plight of a middle-aged actress.

Jana felt even better about that take. Their relationship worked, and the energy bounced back and forth between them almost effortlessly. Again Jana wondered what it would be like sharing her days with Bove and kissing Bove in bed before sleep each night.

Herm's call for action brought Jana back to the scene. Bove's close-up was even better than the first two takes. It was as if they had been married for years with an easygoing yet emotional rapport.

"Cut!"

"Good job, partner."

Bove smiled at Jana. "Right back at you."

As she started to rise from the bed, Jana spotted

Christa in the distance with a look of horror on her face. The young woman screamed as a lighting screen headed straight for her. Stu Silverman, standing next to Christa, noticed and pushed Christa out of the way in the nick of time. The screen crashed to the floor inches away from Christa's feet. Standing on the other side of her, Andrew Bianca took his wife in his arms and she wept on his shoulder.

Bove whispered to Jana, "Here we go again."

Chapter 3

A few minutes later, Christa Bianca rested on the bed used for the scene, with her husband, uncle, and agent surrounding her. The nurse on the set had pronounced her unharmed, at least physically.

With his silver hair and red face, Stu Silverman looked like a Christmas ornament as he shouted at the director, "How could this have happened?"

Herm picked at a pockmark on his cheek. "I talked to the lighting crew, and they said the screen was secure."

"Obviously not, since it came crashing down on my wife," Andrew whined.

Nicholas Hartford placed a hand on his niece's shoulder. "Are you sure you're all right, honey?"

Christa sighed. "I'm fine. The screen didn't touch me."

"Only because I pushed you away." Stu glared at Herm.

Herm said, "We'll be more careful next time."

"I should hope so!" Stu said.

Standing a few feet from the bed, Jana said to Bove, "It wasn't an accident."

Bove replied, "Did someone in your old *Pink Ballerina* movie get hit with a lighting instrument?"

"Very funny." Jana took in the scene of Christa surrounded by the three men in her life with Karen

Evans, the two young couples, and Cindi standing nearby. "I just checked. I've been around lighting equipment for many years. The tripod under the light screen *was* secure. It wouldn't have fallen, unless someone knocked it over."

Bove rubbed the back of his thick neck and his bicep nearly burst out of his turquoise robe. "All the lights were on us. Maybe somebody stumbled in the dark."

"We were shooting. Everybody was still."

Missy appeared. "I took B.J. out when the commotion started."

"Where is he now?" Jana asked.

"With the nurse. I wanted her to take a look at him just in case."

Jana headed for the main meeting room with Missy at her heels. She was relieved when B.J. and the nurse assured her B.J. was fine.

A production assistant whisked Jana away to her dressing room, where the costume woman asked her to change into a hospital gown and white robe. *Not exactly the most glamorous costume I've ever worn on film.* Then she followed the squawking walkie-talkie to a room appointed as a private hospital room.

Bove appeared wearing jeans and a violet V-neck shirt that accentuated his muscles. B.J., wearing adorable feet pajamas, arrived next with Missy. They rehearsed quickly, then after a makeup refresher from Cindi—mostly for Bove, they shot the scene. Hyo, playing an orderly, brought Jana into the room on a gurney then helped her onto the bed. Siobhan, as a nurse, checked Jana's vitals—with the nurse consultant standing off camera ensuring everything was done correctly. Jana pretended she was groggy, as if having just woken from surgery. On the other side of the bed, Alaster, playing the doctor, with Aisha at his side as an intern, offered his prescription of a post-appendectomy hospital stay.

The medical staff left the room. Bove and B.J. each kissed Jana goodnight. Her husband asked her to follow her doctor's orders and said he would be back in the morning. Before they left, B.J. said his line, asking Jana not to be scared in the hospital. Then he ad libbed giving Jana his Clownie rag doll to keep her company without him there. There wasn't a dry eye watching the scene. *That's my boy.*

Herm called out, "Cut!"

Simon started the applause, shouting, "That's my clients!"

After the close-ups were shot, they moved on to rehearse the next scene with Jana alone in her hospital room. Karen Evans, as the night nurse, entered to bring Jana's medications with instructions not to eat anything. Next, Karen asked if Jana's husband was still there. Jana shook her head in a dazed state. Looking down at the folder in her hand, Karen explained she had been trying unsuccessfully to blackmail someone, and she would like to come clean. When Jana pretended to fall asleep, Karen left the folder on the tray table next to Jana's bed. Then Karen left the room. As Jana slept, someone's shadow in the hallway just outside the room raised two hands over Karen's head, sending Karen, or rather her stunt double, crashing to the floor. Finally, with Jana still sleeping off her surgery, Nicholas Hartford walked into the room, took the folder, and fled—with only his arm visible in the shot. After Jana's close-up, Karen had a word with Herm, then he shot the scene again in close-up on Karen.

While the technicians set up for the next scene, Jana noticed Karen speaking to Herm again, then Herm pulling Stu Silverman to a corner of the room.

"Stu, what did you think of Karen's performance?"

The agent shrugged his stooped over shoulders.

"She's got talent."

"Don't they all?"

Herm unleashed a jagged smile. "You should snatch her up before another agent beats you to it."

"I'll take my chances." Stu walked away.

With an eye on the clock, Herm bit at the skin where his fingernails should be and rehearsed the next scene, where Bove and B.J. visit Jana's hospital room the next morning. Jana had the acting challenge of being somewhat drugged, in pain, happy to see her family, experiencing flashbacks about the mysterious folder that came and went from her serving tray—all at the same time. Once Jana's family left, Christa, as the day nurse, entered Jana's room and took her vitals— again with the real nurse off camera coaching Christa through the mechanics of taking Jana's pulse and blood pressure. As in real life, Jana and Christa struck up a friendship.

When they got to Christa's close-up, none of Christa's previous nervousness was visible, and everyone was pleased with each of the takes.

The assistant director shouted, "Lunch!"

Minutes later, Jana and Christa sat on comfortable chairs near the food table in the main meeting room with plates of chicken Caesar salad over napkins on their laps. Jana had settled B.J. down with Missy, playing a card game on the nearby sofa. *Now it's time for a little amateur detecting.* She washed down a bite of salad with a sip of milk. "I enjoyed doing our first scene."

Christa swallowed a large mouthful of her lunch. "It didn't take any acting on my part to enjoy talking with you. I hope we can be friends after this shoot ends, Jana."

"Me too." Jana looked at Christa's nurse's uniform. "I'm sorry you won't get to wear any nice clothes on the show."

Christa laughed. "This beats the clothes I made from cotton fabric on discount back home. Mmm. This salad is delicious." Christa stuffed another large helping into her mouth and talked between bites. "Back home in Renovo, we grew our own fruits and vegetables, and we raised chickens. But what we grew didn't taste *this* good."

Jana looked around the vast room. Bove argued with Karen then stormed out of the room. Karen sat next to Herm on a loveseat near the window, and they made goo-goo eyes at each other over their salad nicoises. "Looks like Karen and Herm are becoming an item."

Christa followed Jana's gaze. "I hope Herm can help Karen get a larger role on her next show."

Seems to me Karen has her clutches set on your role, Christa. "You have a big heart."

"Takes one to know one."

They shared a smile.

Jana spotted Hyo and Aisha sitting opposite Alaster and Siobhan in a corner of the room. "It must be nice for them to work with their partners."

Christa fidgeted in her seat. "I imagine so."

"What's wrong, Christa?"

Christa continued eating her lunch. "They're not exactly…my kind of people."

"What kind of people are they?"

Christa's cheeks flushed. "They arrived here this morning just after Andrew and me. I saw them. I saw what they did."

"What did you see?"

"I don't tell tales out of school, Jana."

Remember what the detective consultant said on Girl Detective. Don't push. Let the interviewee tell you when she's ready.

B.J. shouted, "I won, Mommy!"

"That's wonderful, honey," Jana called out.

Missy said, "Come on, B.J., two out of three."

As B.J. and Missy continued playing, Christa said to Jana, "B.J. is adorable."

"Thank you. My older boys, Devon and Ed, are away with relatives at their lake house."

"I'm sure they're enjoying that. My sisters, brother, and I loved playing at the watering hole when we were kids in Renovo."

"I won again, Missy!" B.J. shouted.

"You sure did, B.J."

"Missy has been a godsend." Jana added, "It isn't easy finding a good nanny nowadays."

Christa's back stiffened.

"Something wrong?"

Christa pulled down the hem of her white skirt. "I'm sure you find me old fashioned, but I was brought up with certain…values."

"Was being a nanny a no-no in your hometown?"

50

"Being a nanny isn't the issue."

"Then what *is* your issue with Missy?"

Christa slid to the edge of her seat. "I know we only met today, but I feel I can trust you."

"You can."

"Then trust me, too." Christa whispered, "Missy should not be around children."

"Why not?"

"Are you a Christian, Jana?"

"Yes."

"Remember when Jesus invited the little children to come to him?"

"Sure. It's a beautiful story."

Her eyes filled with moisture. "Children mean everything to me. Andrew and I haven't been blessed with our own yet, but after my parents passed away, I took care of my younger brother and sisters."

"That's quite admirable. I comforted my younger sister after my mother died." Jana remembered back to the long faces of sad grown-ups, her father weeping, and her younger sister collapsing in her arms. "But thankfully we were well off enough not to have to think about our next meal. It must have been incredibly difficult for you."

"We split the chores. Took work wherever we could get it. Jilly, Todd, and Molly were there for me as much as I was for them. We'd sleep in my momma and daddy's bed together, the four of us, crying the night away. I vowed to do whatever I needed to keep food on the table, pay the bills, and make sure everyone had clothes on their backs."

Jana glanced over at Christa's husband and uncle, sitting on the other side of the room. "Your uncle must have helped."

Christa nodded. "Uncle Nick sent money. I prayed every night that I'd become an actor just like him." She giggled. "I remember during one of his visits, I told Uncle Nick I wanted to be the next Jana Lane, and I asked him if he could help me. He laughed and said there is only one Jana Lane." Tears welled up in her eyes again. "And can you imagine, all these years later, I'm acting with her!"

Jana took in the young woman. "I can see what Andrew and Stu saw in you."

"What's that?"

"Your flawless beauty, talent as an actress, and approachable manner. And how nice for you to have your husband as your manager."

Christa smiled at Andrew. "He's very involved in my career. Is your hubby as well?"

She laughed. "Brian doesn't trust show business and show people. He has his reasons, I guess."

"What reasons?"

"When I was eighteen, I was attacked on the studio lot in LA."

Christa's eyes seemed to double in size. "How horrible! Is that why you stopped acting?"

Jana nodded. "I moved back home to Hyde Park, went to Vassar College, and met Brian. He helped me put the pieces back together."

Christa smiled. "It seems we both married the right man, Jana."

Then why do I keep thinking about Bove? Bove reentered the room, made himself a plate of barley pasta al forno and chard gratin, then sat by the window like a boy whose mother was late picking him up from school.

Back to the investigation. "Christa, I hope Missy meets a nice young man one day, too."

"That's doubtful," Christa replied with a sniff.

"What do you mean?" After a pause, Jana added, "Please tell me."

"That girl is as dangerous as my daddy's rifle when he came home from the gin mill on poker night."

"Why do you dislike Missy? She's my employee. If there's something wrong, I need to know. For my sake as well as B.J.'s."

Christa took in a deep breath. "This morning when I was coming out of the ladies' room, I passed by Missy in the hallway. Please ask Missy about her phone call this morning."

Trying a different tactic, Jana focused her attention on Stu Silverman and Simon sitting on a sofa nearby. Jana noticed Simon eating both his and Stu's turkey salad over mixed greens. "Stu seems to still be upset about the light screen incident."

Christa waved her hand at Jana as if swatting at a persistent moth. "I don't blame the lighting crew. There were so many of us huddled together in the dark section of that small room near all that lighting and sound equipment—watching the amazing Jana Lane in action. Accidents happen. No harm done. Back home I survived when a tree fell near me. Andrew saw the whole thing happen. He said the tree missed me by inches. I can survive a lighting screen."

Jana wiped her mouth with her napkin. "But I looked at the tripod after we finished shooting. That lighting screen was firmly attached, and the tripod had a sandbag over it. I don't see how it could have tipped over unless—"

"Somebody pushed it." Stu Silverman approached them, rubbing his bald head as if a magic ball. "And if I catch whoever tried to hurt my client—accident or not—I'll kill him."

Simon played Robin to Stu's Batman. "I feel the same way about my baby doll."

"Excuse us a moment." Jana grasped Simon's tiny arm and led him toward a private corner of the room. "Simon, you were near Christa when the screen fell on her. Did you see anything?"

"I was standing on the other side of Stu. He's so tall and Christa's so small, I couldn't see much." He snapped his small fingers. "But I *do* remember the two young couples leaving just before that."

"Did they walk by the light screen?"

"I believe so." His eyes rolled around in his head. "And I also remember B.J. standing alone."

"Alone?"

He nodded. "I looked to my other side and B.J. was unattended. I was just about to take his hand when Missy appeared."

"Where had she been?"

He shrugged his small shoulders. "I have three clients. Missy isn't one of them."

Jana and Simon walked back to the easy chairs, where Christa and Stu were in deep discussion.

"I think it's a good project." Stu Silverman played with the gold rings on his fingers.

Simon looked like a dog staring at a doggy treat. "Project?"

Stu smiled revealing jagged yellow teeth. "The next project for Christa. *On My Own* got her a lot of attention."

"An indie film can't hold a candle to the exposure Christa will get guest starring on my baby doll's television series," Simon said as if drawing a line in the sand.

Stu replied, "I wouldn't tie Christa down to a series at her young age." He put his arm around his client's shoulders. "When I discovered Christa in the pageant, I noticed she made some mistakes in how she approached her career. So when I became her agent, Christa started acting Off-Off Broadway then moved to Off Broadway, and finally Broadway. The indie film was next. Now television. And very soon the big studio films." He glowed like a sunrise. "I'll be competing with young A-list agents in Hollywood!"

As Christa calmed the agent waters with Stu and Simon, Jana walked over to Bove. "Karen strikes again?"

Bove stared out the window. Jana followed his gaze to a rainbow presiding over the mountains. "She's staying all week."

"But Karen's wrapped. Nevgere Productions won't pay for her hotel room."

"No, but Herm Fenton will."

Jana sat in the chair opposite his as if knocked off her feet. "Is it because Karen looks like Herm's…friend from LA?"

He looked at her. "Stop being *The Adorable Orphan*. It's because Karen, like Herm's friend, is a good mistress."

"But they just met. How could Karen be Herm's mistress so soon?"

Bove looked at her as if she had said she believed in the Tooth Fairy. "In LA, Karen is known in some quarters as Mistress Wanda with the whip."

Jana did a double-take. "Did Karen ever…?"

He looked like a beagle who just lost his master. "Is that what you think of me?"

"Did you know about this when you married her?"

"Obviously not."

She collapsed back in the easy chair. "I don't know what's obvious anymore. You're married to a whip-cracking mistress. Our director is a masochist. Christa knows something she's not telling about Hyo, Aisha, Alaster, Siobhan, and my son's nanny, which may or may not be why a lighting screen nearly killed Christa. And Detective Bove sits and sulks about his third whack-job wife who got away."

"I'm not a detective anymore. I just play one on TV. And they weren't whack-jobs when I met them."

"Bove, unless you want to spend the rest of your life mooning over duplicitous women, you need to be less capricious about who you ask to marry you."

Bove slid to the edge of his seat. and his pectoral muscles nearly burst out of his shirt. Their knees touched, sending a shiver through her body. "Since we're being honest here, how about taking a look at your own marriage."

"My marriage is fine." *The rare times my husband is in town.*

They were so close his lips nearly touched hers, filling her nostrils with the scent of pine. "Acting is make-believe, Jana. Real life isn't."

"Meaning?"

"You're not a child any longer. It's time to be honest about your real feelings."

"I've never lied to you, or to Brian."

"No, you lied to yourself." He walked out of the room.

Feeling as if caught in a twister, Jana walked on shaky legs to the food table to get a fruit juice. She noticed Missy standing there talking to a tall, thin, young man with carrot-red hair. Jana checked for B.J. who seemed to be having the time of his life hearing a story on Christa's lap.

"What's your name?" The young man scratched at the freckles on his long arms, extending from his pistachio polo shirt.

Missy looked down at her plate. "Missy."

"Hi, Missy. I'm Jason. I'm the props master. The master part makes it sound fancy. It's not really. What I do is bring in, set up, and take away the props." When she looked at him as if he was speaking in another language, Jason added, "Props are things like folders and phones."

"I liked the furniture in the bedroom scenes."

"That's set décor. It can get confusing."

Missy nodded.

He rubbed his long, thin nose. "Are you one of the actresses?"

She shook her head from side to side. "I'm B.J.'s…the little boy's nanny."

"You're so pretty. I thought for sure you were an actress."

She laughed sadly. "I'm just a nanny."

"A nanny's an important job."

"Not really, but I like it."

"So you work for Jana Lane?"

"Um-hm."

Jana positioned herself behind a large grip filling

his plate with roast beef, and she peered around him.

"What's she like?" Jason asked.

"Jana's nice."

"She's a really big star."

"She doesn't act like that."

Phew.

"Do you live in her mansion in Hyde Park?"

Missy nodded. "It's really nice."

"I'll bet. Are you from Hyde Park?"

"Yeah."

"I live with my folks in a small raised ranch in Red Hook. I'd love to have a big house someday, and a family."

"Yeah."

He seems like a nice guy. After what she went through with her ex, the drug addict caveman evangelist, can't she say anything more to Jason than, "Yeah"? And why does she look so morose?

Jason asked, "You like chicken fingers, huh?"

"What?"

He pointed down to Missy's plate.

"Oh. They're for B.J."

"He'll like them. That's one of the nice things about being on a film set. The food is always good. What did *you* have for lunch?"

"I'm not hungry."

"Can I fix you a plate?"

"No, thank you."

"You need to eat." He smiled, revealing a row of straight white teeth. "So you have the energy to take care of B.J."

Smart boy.

Missy nodded. "I'll eat something later."

His aqua eyes danced. "I'll hold you to that, Missy."

She looked away from him.

Jason moved from foot to foot as if standing on hot coals. "Did I say something wrong? Are you okay?"

Missy swallowed hard. "I've had a rough morning."

"Can I do anything to help?"

"There isn't anything you can do. Excuse me." Missy hurried back to B.J. with Jason looking after her like a boy who lost his teddy bear.

Jana picked up a fruit juice container. Noticing the two couples with their heads together at the other end of the table, Jana followed the grip to that end while he filled his plate with potato salad, macaroni salad, and chocolate cake.

"I think we can trust her," Hyo said.

"We can't trust *anyone*," Aisha whispered to her boyfriend.

"She's not only the star, she's the producer." Siobhan placed a pickle on each of their plates. "If word gets out, we could be fired."

Alaster said to his girlfriend, "If only Christa hadn't caught us."

Siobhan rested her plate on the table. "Well, she did. And Christa has been talking to Jana for most of the lunch break."

Aisha's eyes turned to lit coals. "If that bitch tells Jana what we did, I'll wring her neck."

"I don't buy Christa's Daisy Mae act," Sibohan said through gritted teeth.

Hyo folded his arms over his chest. "That's why I think we should tell Jana Lane. As a preemptive strike."

"I agree with Hyo," Alaster said.

Aisha clenched her fists. "None of us are going to tell Jana Lane anything."

"Unless we all agree?"

The other three slowly nodded at Siobhan in agreement.

There's my cue. Jana approached the foursome. "The scenes seem to be going well."

"Yes."

"Sure do."

"Agreed."

"Nice shoot."

Jana smiled back at the two handsome couples. "Thank you for watching my scene with Bove."

"Our pleasure." Aisha wrapped her arm through Hyo's.

Jana continued. "But I noticed you had to leave before the end of the scene."

They shared worried glances. Clearly skilled in improvisation, Siobhan said, "I had an appendicitis attack a few years ago. It was too painful for me to watch yours. It was so realistic, I had to leave."

Hyo nearly fell over from Aisha's poke in his side. "I went after Aisha to make sure she was all right."

"We followed," said Alaster and Siobhan in unison.

And if you believe that, I have a bridge to sell you. "I hope you know I meant what I said this morning. If there is anything you'd like to discuss with me, I am happy to hear it."

They nodded like stuffed animals on a trampoline then moved on to surround Stu Silverman.

Jana helped herself to some yogurt and berries.

Once the foursome had returned to the two loveseats, Jana nearly bumped into Stu who was making a plate of turkey with mixed greens. "Were Hyo, Aisha, Alaster, and Siobhan seeking representation?"

He rubbed his large nose. "Them, Karen Evans, and that has-been Nick who never was anybody— except in the old stories he told his niece. They should all only know an agent in Hollywood is expected to be young nowadays."

"Like an actress."

"Maybe we older folks should stick together." He touched her arm. "Are you happy with Simon as your agent?"

"Simon's been part of my family since I was five years old."

"That's not what I asked."

"Simon is a wonderful agent. I can't imagine ever leaving him."

Stu grinned. "When I found Christa, she was a poor hick who didn't have a clue as to how to become an actress."

"Christa seems to appreciate what you've done for her. Just as I appreciate what Simon has done for me over all these years."

Stu recited as if a sage, "If I can turn a nobody like Christa Bianca into a star, just think what I can do for the one and only Jana Lane."

"And what can you do for *me*?" Jana smelled whiskey as Nicholas Hartford appeared next to Stu. "The offers have been coming in...a bit slowly nowadays, I'm afraid."

"So what else is new, Nick?" Stu started to walk away.

Nick held his arm. "I'm a good actor, Stu. Audiences remember me from the old days." He ran a hand through his silver hair. "And Christa remembers me. It would make her happy if I could get back on top."

Stu laughed. "You were never on top, Nick. Not even in the middle."

"But I'm Christa's uncle."

"So you got this job. But I have the feeling it will be your last." Stu took off with Nick calling after him.

Simon appeared next to Jana. "Stu's lucky the knives are all plastic."

"Were you hiding under the table, Simon?"

"An agent of my caliber wouldn't resort to that!" He adjusted his pink scarf. "I was hiding behind the grip."

"Simon!"

"I got the idea from you, *Girl Detective*."

"Why were you spying on me?"

"Any agent would do the same when another agent approaches his client like a shark facing a suicidal sea lion."

"Did I prove my loyalty?"

"You certainly did, baby doll." He kissed her cheek. "But if Stu Silverman tries to steal my client again, he's going to have to answer to Simon Huckby." Simon threw back his shoulders, pointed his chin to the cracked ceiling, and headed for Stu like a gunfighter in the old West.

Jana joined B.J. and Missy for a game of cards. She couldn't help overhearing Christa and Andrew talking on the sofa nearby.

"But Stu has worked for years to make this happen

for me." Christa added, "I can't fire him now."

Andrew replied in his nasal twang, "Then let *me* do it."

Christa held his hand. "Honey, I'll always be grateful to Stu for seeing…whatever he saw in that chubby, buck-toothed, hick girl back in Renovo. He taught me so many things, and what he couldn't, he hired others to show me. I can't turn my back on him now that things are looking up for me and Stu's getting on in years."

Andrew pouted like a kid facing coal at Christmas. "I'm your husband and your manager. I don't see why you need an agent."

"To save me from falling light screens, for one."

He wrapped his thin arms around her. "I was so scared, baby. I don't know what I'd do without you."

The assistant director shouted, "Lunch hour is over in five, folks!"

There was pandemonium in the room as everyone raced to the table for a last minute snack.

B.J. said, "Mommy, I want a cookie."

Jana's maternal lioness kicked in and she battled her way through the crowd to bring her son and Missy a cookie. As B.J. ate both of them, Jana noticed Stu, Simon, Nick, Christa, and Andrew in a corner of the room eating quickly. She walked over before any blood was shed. "You two sharing agent notes?"

Stu rested his half-eaten plate on a side table. "I don't feel too good."

Sounding like Bette Davis, Simon said, "What a pity!"

"You don't have to watch my scenes, Stu." Christa added, "Lie down on the sofa if you like."

Andrew glared at Stu. "At your age, you should take a nap in the afternoon."

A production assistant appeared. "Jana and Christa, please come with me."

The young man led them to a room set up as an office. Jana waited out in the hallway, as Herm shot the scene where Christa unlocks a file cabinet and accidentally finds the telling folder.

Jana followed them to the nearby room set up as Jana's hospital room. She took off her robe and hopped back into the bed, wearing her hospital gown. Christa sat in a chair at her bedside and they rehearsed the scene where Christa confides to Jana that someone at the hospital is selling organs of deceased patients for profit. They also discussed the death of Nurse One, deemed an accident.

As Cindi refreshed her makeup, Jana followed Cindi's gaze at Bove standing in the shadows. Jana also noticed the two couples, Karen, Jason, Missy, B.J., Andrew, Simon, and Stu ready to watch the shooting. Jana couldn't help notice that Stu was sweating profusely, breathing deeply, and rubbing his arm.

Simon asked Stu, "Are you all right?"

Stu replied, "I can't see so good."

"We're in the dark," Simon replied.

Jana and Christa performed the scene, which ended with a shot of Nick listening at the door—again only showing Nick's arm to keep the viewers in suspense about the identity of the murderer. As they shot Jana's close-up, Jana wasn't surprised at the rapport the two actresses had in the scene, or how easily Christa was in touch with her emotions. When they shot Christa's close-up, Jana couldn't take her eyes off the young woman. Every move Christa made and every word she said exuded honesty and reality. *It's obvious what Stu Silverman saw in young Christa Bianca back in Renovo, Pennsylvania.* Jana totally believed Christa was a frightened nurse coming to the detective's wife for help. *Or was Christa herself really frightened?*

Following two more takes, the scene came to an end and Herm yelled, "Cut!" As lights, chatter, and movement filled the room, Jana noticed Stu Silverman gasping for air.

Bove hurried over to Stu. "Do you need help?"

Stu reeled from side to side like a hit bowling pin. "I...I..." He vomited on Bove's tassel loafers then collapsed at Bove's feet.

Chapter 4

A half hour later, Jana sat next to Bove in the front row of a lecture hall once used by the hospital, no doubt to keep doctors abreast of the latest treatments for tuberculosis. Jana had sent Missy and B.J. home in a taxi. The rest of the cast and crew were dispersed throughout the raked seating area.

Still the detective, Bove asked her, "What did you see?"

Jana whispered in his ear and enjoyed his thick hair brushing against her cheek. "Stu was poisoned."

He leaned in and their shoulders touched, sending a shiver down her spine. "By whom?"

"Someone in the cast or crew."

"That narrows it down. You're slipping, *School Spy*."

"It's as big a field as your ex-girlfriends."

Lieutenant Mario Rivera stood at the front of the room looking officious in a dark suit. He scratched at his curly black hair sending a windstorm of dandruff onto the podium before him. "May I have everyone's attention?" When the crowd quieted down, he motioned to Christa Bianca, sitting between her husband and her uncle. She wept into Andrew's chest as Nick patted her back. "My condolences, Mrs. Bianca, for your loss."

"Thank you." Christa blew her nose.

"Once the autopsy has been completed, Mr.

Silverman's body will be flown to his daughter in Fort Worth, Texas, for immediate burial. The room where Mr. Silverman took ill has been taped off. Due to this tragic incident, your director has decided to suspend shooting for the rest of the day."

Herm rose from his chair next to Karen Evans. "But be here bright and early tomorrow morning and ready to work."

"How did Stu die?" Nicholas Hartford asked with the projection of a one-time stage actor.

Rivera offered a patronizing smile. "We haven't completed our investigation, but given Mr. Silverman's age and according to his doctor, Mr. Silverman's status as suffering from heart disease, my assumption is that Mr. Silverman passed away due to a heart attack." Once the chatter subsided, he said, "Officer Fierst will move through the rows to ask your name and place of residence while here in Hyde Park. After we receive that information, you may go. I have an officer stationed at the entrance of this building. No reporters will be permitted inside and you may not under any circumstances speak with any member of the press. Please leave that to me. Thank you."

As private conversations commenced, he walked over to Jana. "We meet again, Mrs. Otley."

Jana and Bove rose to their feet. "Detective Rivera, this is Detective Bove."

Bove shook Rivera's hand. "Ex-detective."

"And ex-football player," Rivera replied as if he had eaten sour milk and sardines.

So it isn't only actresses that Rivera frowns upon. "Bove plays my co-star in the television show."

"Of course." Rivera smirked as if he had been told

they were from outer space. "Mrs. Otley, I want to ask you not to meddle in this investigation, as you have done in the past."

You mean when I solved the cases you couldn't?

Bove cleared his throat. "Detective, I think you should hear Jana out."

Rivera sighed. "Do you have something you'd like to tell me, Mrs. Otley?"

"As a matter of fact, I do, Detective."

"I was afraid of that. Please, follow me."

A few moments later, they assembled in a small room appointed as an office set for the show. Rivera sat behind the narrow oak desk, and Bove and Jana sat on upright chairs opposite him. Rivera took a small pad and pencil from his inside jacket pocket. "What is it you would like to tell me?" He scratched his head with the pencil and covered the desk in white.

Jana sat at the edge of her seat. "Stu Silverman was poisoned with hemlock and oleander."

"And you know this how?"

Jana explained, "The villain in *The Cutest Scientist* used those poisons on Timmy. I figured it out and saved him."

Rivera looked at her as if she'd said animals could talk. "And you saw these herbs on Stu Silverman's plate?"

She nodded.

"I'll speak to the caterer."

"The caterer won't know anything about this."

Rivera looked at Jana like a school principal with a truant.

"The herbs were never in the salad on the food table. They were put in Stu's plate afterward."

"Then why didn't you stop him from eating them?"

"After Stu collapsed, I went back into the main room and looked at his plate. He had left it on a side table. There were a few sprigs left on the plate."

Rivera sighed. "Why don't you tell me your theory from the beginning?"

She rested back in her chair. "During lunchtime in the large room set up as our sitting room, Stu made a plate for himself of turkey and mixed greens. I watched him and there were no suspicious greens on his plate at that time. However, when the A.D.—"

"A.D.?"

"—Assistant Director called five minutes left for lunch, everyone milled around the room frantically grabbing a last bite or drink. It must have been at that time when someone dropped the herbs onto Stu's plate, and he ate them without realizing it." Jana tented her fingers. "I remember the poison consultant on the set of *The Cutest Scientist* telling me the symptoms of hemlock and oleander poisoning generally begin thirty minutes after ingestion."

"What are the symptoms?" Bove asked, clearly reverting back to detective mode.

Jana replied, "Nausea, vomiting, sore muscles, sweating, and vision loss. The same symptoms Stu experienced while we shot the scene in the room set up as my hospital room. So anyone could have poisoned him."

Rivera wrote a note. "We will test Mr. Silverman's food."

"By now the murderer must have removed the poison from the plate."

"We'll look for any residue on the plate, and for

poison in the autopsy." Rivera ran a hand through his hair and dandruff flew in all directions like a snowstorm. "Who do you believe did this and why?"

Jana did a double-take. "You're asking *me*?"

Rivera said to Bove, "Mrs. Otley seems to have a flair for this sort of thing."

"You're telling me." Bove winked at Jana.

Thinking, Jana said, "I need time to investigate."

Rivera snapped his pad shut and dandruff flew across the room. "I was afraid you would say that. Please let *me* do the investigating, Mrs. Otley."

Jana, Bove, and Rivera returned to the lecture hall, finding Christa, Andrew, and Nick huddled together near the doorway. Jana said, "I'm so sorry, Christa." *What is it about you that makes me feel like I'm with the daughter I never had?*

"Stu was the first person who really believed in me, Jana." Christa blinked back tears. "If it wasn't for him, I'd probably be homeless in Renovo."

Andrew stroked her hair. "Don't worry, baby. I'll be your manager *and* your agent now."

Nick added, "And I'll help in any way I can. We'll be a team on screen like Jana was with her father."

Andrew grimaced.

"You're both so good to me." Christa let the tears flow.

Jana said, "Christa, I have reason to believe Stu's lunch was poisoned."

"Poisoned?" Christa's face drained of color.

Jana nodded. "Did you happen to see anything or anyone that looked out of the ordinary regarding Stu's lunch?"

Lines formed on Christa's smooth forehead. "At

the five-minute call, we all went to the food table for seconds then returned to the sofa. I was talking to Andrew. At one point I put down my plate. So did Stu. Right next to mine." Her eyes doubled in size. "Stu and I had the same lunch. What if he picked up my plate by mistake?"

Andrew gasped. "You think the poison could have been meant for Christa!"

Rivera said, "We will investigate this thoroughly. You have my assurance."

Once Jana had calmed Christa and Andrew down, Andrew led his wife away.

Simon appeared at Jana's side. "Are you all right, baby doll?"

"I'm fine." She looked after Christa. "Obviously Christa isn't."

"It's a terrible thing to lose an agent." He wrapped his thin arms around Jana and Bove. "Aren't you two glad you will never have to experience it? Nothing can kill me."

The car from the production company drove Jana back to her mansion. She hurried up the spiral stairs to B.J.'s room, where she found her son taking a nap. Jana couldn't resist kissing his pink cheeks and covering B.J. with his dancing elephant sheet. Missy stood at the window wiping away the tears on her cheeks then tossing her tissues into the wastebasket shaped like a giraffe.

It's time for some girl talk. "Follow me."

Missy followed Jana into the cerise sitting room down the hall. Once they were seated on blue wingback chairs with rose inlay, Jana took the girl's hands in hers. "Missy, I know something is wrong. I'd like you to trust me, and tell me what is bothering you."

Tears filled Missy's dark eyes.

"Is there a problem with the house? With B.J.? With me?"

"No. I really like working here. B.J. is such a sweet boy. And being on the movie set was amazing."

Until someone was murdered. "Then what is it?"

"I'm fine. Really."

"No, you aren't, Missy. And I need you to tell me why."

Missy looked away.

"Before the lighting screen fell on set today, why did you leave B.J.?"

"I took a walk."

"I don't think that's true. I think you left because you were upset, and I'd like to know why."

Missy rested her head in her hands.

"Earlier today you were also in the hospital hallway—to make a phone call. Christa came out of the ladies' room and overheard your call."

Rage filled Missy's face. "Unfortunately."

"Who were you talking to on the phone?"

Missy looked down at the rug.

"Missy, please tell me."

"My doctor."

"Are you ill?"

"I don't feel ill."

"Then why did you call your doctor."

Missy swallowed hard. "It's personal."

"Was it to get test results?"

Missy nodded.

Her ex-boyfriend was a drug addict. "Missy, did you take the new blood test for the AIDS virus?"

Missy burst into tears. "I don't want anyone to know!"

"Fine, but I'm your employer…and your friend. I want to help you, but I can't do that unless you tell me what's going on."

Missy nodded, took in a deep, shaky breath, and pulled back her shoulders. "I've been feeling run down and achy. It took me longer than usual to get over my last cold. When I told my doctor, he ordered the test. He said I have the virus that causes AIDS. That Matty gave it to me. I'm only twenty-five. I don't want to die!"

Jana wrapped her arms around the girl. "You won't die, Missy. Your doctor caught it early. There are new drugs."

"My doctor said they all have bad side effects."

"What is your T-cell count?"

"Five hundred and fifty."

"Good. Let's work to keep that up."

Missy stood and held onto the teakwood desk nearby. "I know this means I can't be B.J.'s nanny any longer."

Jana stood next to her. "Your HIV status means no such thing. AIDS isn't transmitted by touch or breath."

"But what if I accidentally cut myself and some of my blood gets on B.J.?"

"You'll be careful that won't happen."

Missy did a double-take. "Do you mean I don't have to leave?"

"That's exactly what I mean."

Missy threw her arms around Jana. "Thank you so much, Jana. I'll wear rubber gloves when I touch B.J. And I'll be careful not to cut myself."

"Missy, all I ask is that you take care of yourself.

Eat well, exercise, get plenty of rest, keep your stress level down, do what your doctor tells you, and talk to someone for support."

"I don't have anybody to talk to."

"You have me. And you have the young prop man."

Missy laughed bitterly. "I made a total fool of myself with Jason today. I doubt he'll talk to me again."

"I think you're wrong. Give him a chance tomorrow. Will you do that, Missy?"

"All right." Missy took Jana's hands. "Thank you. You really practice divine hospitality like Reverend Heather says at church." She grimaced. "Unlike Christa Bianca who calls herself a Christian."

Jana sat Missy on a burgundy-colored loveseat in the shape of a heart. "What did Christa say to you in the hallway today after she overheard you on the phone with your doctor?"

"That she was sorry I have AIDS, but I should know it's God's wrath against sinners like homosexuals and drug addicts."

"When I told her I'm not either of those things, she said, since I'm a fornicator, I'm going to Hell anyway." Missy wept into her hands.

Jana put her arm around the girl. "You aren't going to Hell, Missy. Christa is no doubt parroting rhetoric from some fire and brimstone dinosaur raising tax-exempt money on the misfortunes of others."

"I can't believe this happened to me. I thought only homosexuals got AIDS."

"In Africa, where it began, the disease has mostly been contracted by heterosexual men and women. And many children, too. I don't believe in a God that creates disease to punish anyone." She looked out the window at the azure sky surrounding the kelly-green lawn. "President Reagan and Congress are dragging their heels on providing funding while infection rates rise steadily. I can't help thinking more would be done in this country if wealthy straight people were the targets of the disease."

"Dr. Sherman said he could get me into a new clinical trial to hopefully extend the time before I get sick. He said the drug is very expensive, but the medicine would be free for as long as I was in the study."

"That's good, Missy."

She nodded. "But he said many people can't afford that drug, or any of the others. And they can't get into a trial or study. So those people are dying."

Jana sank back into the loveseat. "How awful."

"I read about your fundraisers for AIDS in Hyde Park, New York City, and Washington, DC."

Jana sighed. "I wish I could do more."

Missy bit her lip. "I remember reading in a movie magazine about a celebrity who had a foundation to help kids with cancer. The foundation raised money for research, treatment, drugs, clinical trials, even housing near hospitals for the patients' loved ones. I wish there was something like that for AIDS."

Yes! The Jana Lane Foundation for people with AIDS. "Missy, you're a genius."

"What did I say?"

"You said a great deal. Now go look in on B.J. I have a phone call to make."

Jana raced down the hallway to her bedroom. She sat on the gold-trimmed white chaise and picked up the matching French Provincial phone. "Simon, I have a task for you and Cornelius."

Her agent sighed so heavily, Jana's hair nearly fanned out. "If it's to gather entertainment for another one of your AIDS fundraisers by this weekend, you have the wrong number, baby doll."

"Simon, would I ask you to do something like that?"

"Yes, and you have—three times!"

"I don't want you to produce another large fundraiser."

"But?"

"I want you to produce a series of variety shows, and send them out on the road to tour theaters as fundraisers for AIDS. I'll pay all production costs. Please ask my publicist to take care of publicity. Also, please set up a meeting with my lawyer to turn the legal wheels for the new Jana Lane AIDS Foundation. And arrange for television and radio interviews. I'd like to start with my first interview as soon as possible. Oh, and let's have a big dinner dance fundraiser kick-off this Friday night. Book all the pavilions at Bowdoin Park. It's so lovely there overlooking the mountains. Cornelius' orchestra can play. Use whichever caterer you like."

What came into her phone's earpiece sounded like a wounded animal next to a skidding car as a hoard of spectators shrieked in horror. "Did a light screen fall on *you* after I left the shoot today? How do you expect me to do all that?"

"Very well as usual, Simon. And Cornelius can help you."

He sighed. "You'll be the death of me, baby girl."

"As you said, you're immortal. Love you, Simon."

Next, Jana called Devon and Ed between their sailboat races at the lake. They assured her they were having the time of their lives, eating well, obeying Jackson, and sleeping between pillow fights with Tyler and Topher. When a water pistol invasion occurred, the two boys bid her adieu.

Finally, Jana curled up on the lounge, and phoned Brian in Tampa. "How's the sexiest architect in Florida?"

"Only in *Florida*? Hi, babe."

It's so good to hear your voice. "You sound tired."

Brian exhaled loudly. "It's been constant meetings since I arrived."

Come home. "Are things going smoothly?"

He laughed. "Things never go smoothly with new mall construction."

"I have faith in you."

"That's because I'm so cute."

"No arguments here."

"How's B.J.?"

"Taking a nap, and loving every minute of being a TV star."

"Like mother, like son."

True. "I called Devon and Ed."

"Me too."

"Should we be worried that they don't miss us?"

"They'll realize they miss us—when they get back home."

I miss you so much.

"How was your first day on the job?"

Jana used her acting skills to lighten her voice. "Fine. We're shooting at the abandoned TB hospital in town. The director, Herm Fenton, is a bit curt, but skilled. The leading guest star, Christa Bianca, and I hit it off right away."

"You're a great actress, babe, but I'm your husband, remember? And I have a meeting in ten minutes. So, let me take a deep breath and give me my medicine."

"I don't know what you're talking about, Brian." *Did I sound like a society matron?*

"Cut to the chase, babe."

"The chase?"

"Let's start with, who's your leading man?"

"He-he's a f-fine a-actor." *Am I stuttering?*

"What's his name, Jan?"

"That's a funny story."

"I'm sure it's hysterical."

"The producers wanted to add a realistic touch to the show, so they cast a real detective."

"No."

"And since he's an ex-football star, I guess they think his name will help with the ratings."

"Not him."

"And he's been studying acting."

"It's Chris Bove!"

"Simon is his agent."

"I don't care if Mother Theresa is his agent. That guy kissed you in DC!"

"It was just one little kiss when we went out dancing."

"I have to go."

"Why?"

"I'm phoning the hotel doctor for ulcer medicine."

"Bove and I work well together. And aren't you

glad a real detective is watching over me on set and here at home?"

"Here at home?"

She laughed too grandly. "Bove is going through a divorce. His ex-wife is in the cast. She's staying at the hotel, and he's living in our guest cottage. Didn't I mention that?"

"You forgot that part."

Jana bit a nail. "Brian, please trust me."

"I trust you. It's Bove I don't trust."

"He's a good guy. And I can handle him."

"Like you handle me?"

"Very differently. You're the only guy for me."

"I'll hold you to that when I get home."

"I hope so. When will that be by the way?"

"In a few days hopefully, maybe longer. I can't leave here until everything is going well."

Jana kissed the phone. "I love you so much."

"I love you more." He kissed back.

"Well, I'll let you go to your meeting."

"Not so fast. Spill it."

"Spill what?"

"You know what. Who was murdered on the set today?"

Is my husband a psychic? "How did you know?"

"Somebody got killed?"

"Just one person. The other person had a near miss."

He groaned. "On the set where my wife and son are working!"

"Christa's agent caught the lighting screen before it hit Christa. Then someone laced her or Stu's salad with poison herbs, which Stu ate."

"Where were you and B.J. when this happened?"

"I was in bed with Bove, and B.J. was with his new nanny, who ran out into the hall upset about finding out she has AIDS. So I'm going to start an AIDS foundation to raise money."

"Stop! I don't want to hear anymore."

"Don't you want the list of suspects?"

"No. I just want to hear you promise me you'll find the murderer soon." His voice broke. "And you won't let anything happen to you…or to our son."

"I promise, Brian."

"*And* that you both will be waiting for me when I get home."

"With open arms." Jana heard noise on the other end of the phone.

"I have to go."

"You're always in my mind and heart, Brian."

"You're my salvation, babe. Take care of the people I love most in the world."

"I will."

Jana hung up the phone and wiped a tear from under her eye. The phone rang. "Yes?"

"The kitchen in the guest house is too small."

"Beggars can't be choosers, Bove."

"Let's go out to dinner."

"No dancing?"

"Not tonight. I'll treat."

"Do you have enough money after all your failed weddings?"

"I think I can swing dinner. When should I pick you up?"

"How about six?"

"See you then."

Jana changed into sweat clothes, worked out in her home gym to REO Speedwagon's "Can't Fight This Feeling," got B.J. his dinner, bathed and dressed him for bed, then read him a bedtime story about clowns.

When Missy relieved her, Jana took a bath in her circular tub with gold falcon faucets surrounded by wall-to-wall mirrors, and relaxed into the warm scents of lavender, lemon balm, and chamomile. Then she dressed in a coral chemise sleeveless dress with matching strappy boots, bag, earrings, eye shadow, rouge, and lipstick. She teased and layered her hair, making a fan around her face.

At six on the dot, the doorbell rang. Jana quickly checked in on B.J. and Missy then hurried down the spiral staircase and opened the double doors to Bove. Nearly drooling on her saffron marble floor, Jana held onto the grandfather clock for support. She gazed at Bove in a teal T-shirt, white parachute pants and blazer with his dark hair slicked back off his handsome face.

"Stop gaping at me."

"I'm not *gaping* at you." *That was pretty unconvincing for an actress.* "I was…admiring my…stained glass window."

The ex-detective clearly didn't buy it. "You look very nice, too."

"Thank you."

"That's how normal people do it. Let's go."

Following a brief ride in Bove's sports car, Jana sat opposite Bove in an Italian restaurant that could have been in Tuscany. They were surrounded by gold-framed paintings of villas on rolling hills, bowls of grapes, jugs of wine, and couples gazing at earth-toned sunsets. Bove looked even better in candlelight than under the television set lighting. Sitting in a portico with a view of the mountains, Jana struggled to concentrate on her red wine and eggplant rollatini appetizer. "This is delicious."

Bove tasted his *pasta e fagioli* then sat still with his eyes closed. "This could use a bit more garlic."

"Does your brother make that in your parents' restaurant in DC?"

"My guess is he makes Allison mostly."

"Now who mentioned Allison?"

"*Touché.*" He clicked his wine glass against hers and they drank.

Jana asked, "How are things with Karen?"

He sat back in his chair. "We both agree on one thing. We want a speedy divorce." He winked at her. "Then I'll be free to marry you."

"Three strikes and you're out, Bove. I'll stick with my soulmate."

"Maybe that's the secret to a successful marriage."

She raised an eyebrow. "Do tell."

"See your spouse as little as possible."

"Brian and I see each other a great deal. And I miss him terribly when we aren't together." *Which seems to be more and more lately.*

"I don't miss Karen." He continued eating. "Thanks for letting me use the guest cottage."

"Even though the kitchen is too small?"

"The kitchen's fine. I just used that as an excuse to take you out to dinner."

"I'm flattered."

The busboy cleared their plates. "Excuse me, are you Jana Lane?"

"Yes."

"Could I bother you for an autograph?"

"Sure." She dug into her purse for a pen.

"Would you sign your napkin to Vinnie?"

Jana signed and handed the young man her napkin.

"Thank you so much!"

"My pleasure, Vinnie."

Once he was gone, Jana said, "Now I don't have a napkin."

"The price of fame."

The waiter served their entrées: parmesan crusted chicken with fettucine and broccoli for Bove, and sea bass in marinara sauce over whole wheat linguini and spinach for Jana.

Jana let a bite of the delicious meal melt on her tongue. "Wonderful."

Bove tasted his. "A tad too much parsley in mine."

She put down her fork. "Bove, you didn't ask me out to dinner to talk about garlic and parsley, or to gaze at me over the candlelight. You miss being a detective, and you want to go over the suspects and clues with me for Stu's murder."

"That's my girl." He winked. "I agree with you by the way—that Stu Silverman was murdered."

She continued eating her dinner. "Explain."

"Stu was Christa Bianca's agent. I'm thinking whoever tried to kill Christa, went after Stu for saving her."

Jana slid to edge of her seat. "I was thinking the same thing. There's no way that light screen could have fallen unless somebody knocked it over. Had it not been for Stu, Christa would no longer be with us."

"And now Stu is no longer with us."

"And Stu also discovered Christa, paid for her

lessons and entry to Hollywood, planned her career when she was fumbling in the dark, and by all intents and purposes had everything mapped out for her to become a very big star."

A crease formed between Bove's eyebrows. "Who wouldn't want that?"

Jana took a sip of wine. "Pretty much everyone at the shoot today."

"Walk me through it."

"The two couples have something against Christa, but I'm not sure what it is. They also asked Stu to be their agent, and he declined. Nicholas Hartford did as well."

"As did Karen—via Herm."

"I thought Simon got Karen this job."

"He did, because I asked him to. Simon wants nothing to do with Karen as a client." He swallowed hard. "Smart man." He spoke with his mouthful. "And an angry man, after Stu tried to steal you away from him."

Jana waved him away like smoke. "Simon would never hurt anyone unless…"

"Unless 'anyone' was trying to take Jana Lane away from him? Simon was pretty close to Christa when the screen fell, and he was eating lunch near Stu this afternoon."

She wouldn't allow herself to think that her mentor and friend could be involved in murder. "Everyone was hurrying around after Herm called five minutes. Anyone could have dropped those herbs on Stu's plate—or Christa's plate right next to it."

"Which brings us to Christa's husband and her uncle."

Jana washed down her food with a sip of wine. "Christa and Andrew were childhood sweethearts, and Andrew paid for her to enter the beauty pageant. He sure seems possessive of her."

"Brian isn't possessive of you?"

"No." *Except when I'm surrounded by murder.*

"I'd be possessive if we were married."

She enjoyed his thick, strong hand over hers. *Don't go there, girl.* She freed her hand. "No thanks. I've seen your record with wives, Bove. Besides, we're talking about Christa, not me. I like her a great deal, but we're very diffcrent."

"How so?"

"Unlike me, Christa was brought up poor, called 'Rag Doll' as a girl, raised her brother and sisters, and started her career when she was a young adult."

"But *like* you, Christa is gorgeous, a great actress, loves kids, and has a soft spot for the men in her life." His eyes begged for affection.

Back to the investigation. "Which brings us to Uncle Nick who Christa looked up to as a child, and she recently got him this job."

"Like Andrew, Nick seems to want Christa all to himself."

"There's also Karen who wants Christa's role on the show, and Herm who seems to be wrapped around his mistress' little finger."

"Or her big whip."

"Not to mention my new nanny who had a disagreement with Christa."

He finished the last of his dinner. "About what?"

"A personal issue." *Which Christa and I will definitely discuss.*

"Keep your secret, Jana. Just let me know what it is before your nanny commits the next murder."

"Missy isn't the murderer."

"She looks pretty suspicious to me. So does her boyfriend, the prop guy."

"What's suspicious about Jason?"

"He seems to be watching everyone." He smiled. "Like you watch me."

She returned the smile. "I want to make sure you don't meet another woman who is wrong for you."

"How about a woman who is *right* for me?"

Okay heartbeat, calm down to rapid. "Cindi seems to like you."

"She's a nice woman. But she's not Jana Lane."

Though Jana wasn't finished with her dinner, Bove motioned to the waiter for the check. He paid it then said, "Let's go."

"Where?"

"For a walk."

That's one way to keep my figure.

Jana and Bove walked along the green lawn surrounding the restaurant, watching the sun set ribbons of gold, indigo, and tangerine through the mountains. He took her hand. "I've missed you."

She couldn't deny it. "I've missed you, too."

They stopped at a bench next to a lamppost. Bove said, "Stay close to me on set tomorrow."

"Do you need protection, Bove?"

"I don't want anything to happen to you."

"Nothing bad will happen to me. Now that you're here."

"Rivera doesn't seem like he'll be much help."

"No, it's up to us to figure this out, Bove."

They walked to Bove's car, and he drove Jana back to her mansion.

Upon arriving home, Jana checked in with Missy, kissed sleeping B.J., and washed and put on a beige satin nightgown. She climbed into bed and rested her head on the fluffy, soft pillow. Turning onto her side, Jana's arm rubbed against her chest. *What was that?* She reached through the V-neck of her nightgown and examined her breast. *It's a lump!*

Chapter 5

The office door opened, and Jana Lane held her breath. Light spilled into the dark room from the hallway, and a shadow approached the desk. Sweat soaked Jana's neck as she heard voices coming from the hall. The shadow opened the door and left. With her heart in her throat, Jana crawled out from behind the desk, opened the door, and peered out from side to side. She exhaled deeply, realizing the hallway was empty. As she left the room and walked cautiously down the hallway, Jana heard footsteps behind her drawing menacingly close.

Jana woke the next morning having slept only a couple of hours. She did some yoga deep breathing in bed. Once she calmed down from her nightmare—and from the discovery of the lump in her breast—she put on sweat clothes and worked out in her home gym. Next, she took a shower. *The lump is still there.* Talking herself out of panicking, she sat on her chaise and phoned her doctor's receptionist to make an appointment. *Now to get through until my appointment tomorrow.* Jana dressed in a pink ruffled blouse, white slacks, and a pink jacket with shoulder pads. She added gold leaf earrings and a matching necklace. Once she had gone over her lines for the day's shooting, she got B.J. up, washed, and dressed. As Theresa took her post in front of the television set in the kitchen, Jana, Missy,

B.J., and Bove herded into the waiting car. Within minutes they were back in the large meeting room at the hospital.

Once they had eaten breakfast, Jana and B.J. got into makeup and wardrobe: a polo shirt and chinos for B.J., and the hospital gown and robe for Jana. Though her costume wasn't very flattering, it was comfortable.

Back in the main meeting room, B.J. and Missy sat on a sofa playing a board game about clowns, and Jana cased the crowded room. Christa and Andrew weren't there. *Christa is probably still in makeup with Andrew guarding her.* Herm and Karen sat on a loveseat in one corner of the room. The two couples were nestled together in another area. Bove, looking delicious in a lemon polo shirt and black slacks, stood near the window talking to Nicholas Hartford and Simon—who blew her a kiss. *Good luck interrogating Nick, Bove.* Jana's eyes locked with Jason's across the room. *Is he scanning the room, too?*

Jana walked over to the buffet table. "I don't believe we've met. I'm Jana Lane."

Jason wiped his hands on his sweatshirt then again on his jeans. "It's a pleasure to meet you, Miss Lane."

As they shook hands, Jana said, "Please, call me Jana."

"I will." Jason scratched at his auburn hair. "I'm Jason Franks...the prop master."

"I know. My son's nanny, Missy, met you yesterday."

He swooned. "Missy's a nice girl."

"Yes, she is. Are you from around here, Jason?"

"I'm from Red Hook." He rubbed his long nose.

Did it grow? "How did Nevgere Productions find

you?"

"I found *them*. I applied for the position from an ad in the newspaper."

"So, this is your first job with them?"

He nodded. "Hopefully it will be my last—when the show is a big hit and runs for years."

Jana took a small fruit juice container from the table. "Have you met the other actors?"

"No. They don't seem interested in talking to a lackey." He smiled. "Missy said you were different. She's right." Jason blushed.

"Thank you." She spotted Christa and Andrew headed their way. "I'll introduce you to Christa Bianca."

The color drained from his young face.

"Are you all right?"

Jason spoke quickly. "That was horrible about what happened to her agent yesterday. The ticker can go at any minute, especially when you get older."

Christa, in her nurse's uniform, and Andrew, in a shiny dark suit, stood next to Jana. "It's so good to see you," Christa said, giving Jana a big hug.

Jana asked, "Are you feeling better today, Christa?"

"I cried myself to sleep last night in Andrew's arms. I just can't believe Stu is gone. He's been with me for seven years." Tears brimmed in Christa's eyes. "You said someone put poison in the food. Why would someone do that?"

Jana replied, "That's what Detective Rivera is trying to find out."

Christa wiped her eyes with a tissue. "Stu was like a father to me."

I feel the same way about Simon.

"I'll be her agent now," Andrew said in his nasal twang, pushing his glasses up the bridge of his nose.

Christa said, "Agent, manager, and husband all rolled into one."

"And watchdog," Andrew added.

Christa kissed Andrew's cheek. "What would I do without this man?"

"You'll never have to find out." Andrew hugged Christa into his thin chest.

Jana remembered Jason was standing with them. "Christa and Andrew, this is Jason Franks, our prop master."

Jason offered his hand. Instead of shaking it, Christa stared at him. "You look awfully familiar. Have we met somewhere before?"

"I don't think so." Jason shuffled from one work boot to the other.

Andrew shook Jason's hand. "Given what happened yesterday with the light screen, I'd appreciate it if you make sure there are no more accidents."

Jason cleared his throat. "There'll be no accidents with props. I promise you that."

"Good."

Christa stared at Jason again. "You were dressed differently, but I'm sure we met. Have you ever been to Renovo, Pennsylvania?"

"I've never left the Hudson Valley, New York," Jason replied.

I can tell he's lying.

Nicholas Hartford, in a gray three-piece suit, approached them. He coiled an arm around Christa. "Here's my lovely niece. Are you feeling better this morning, honey?"

Andrew took her hand. "Christa's fine."

She kissed Nick's cheek. "I'm sorry I gave everyone a scare, Uncle Nick. Stu was my mentor."

"You still have me, honey."

She blinked back tears. "Thank goodness for that."

Andrew grimaced. "Let's get you to makeup."

Christa replied, "I was already there."

"You've been crying, baby. You need a touch up." Andrew led Christa out of the room.

"I'll join them." Nick winked at Jana. "At my age, I need all the help I can get." He followed them.

Missy, wearing a white blouse and navy blue skirt, tapped Jana's shoulder. "I went over B.J.'s lines with him."

Jana smiled. "He's a quicker study than his mother." She looked at the empty sofa. "Where is he?"

"Bove took him to the bathroom. B.J. told him Clownie had to go. B.J. seems to really like Bove. He's been calling him, 'Dad.'"

On the other side of Jana, Jason stood up straight and unleashed a white smile. "Hiya, Missy."

"Hi, Jason."

"Back again today?" Beads of sweat lined his smooth forehead.

Missy looked down at the floor. "Yeah."

"I checked the props on set." Receiving no response from Missy, Jason added, "The desk in the office needed a calendar, folders with papers in them, a clock, a phone that doesn't need to ring, a framed photograph of a wife and kids, and some pens. Jana's hospital room needed balloons, flowers, and water." He looked to Jana for help.

Jana picked up her cue. "Isn't that interesting, Missy?"

Missy nodded.

"I'll bet you're learning a great deal about television," Jana said.

Missy replied, "Yeah."

Thankfully Missy isn't our scriptwriter. "Missy, you and Jason both grew up in this area. Did you go to the same high school?"

Jason said quickly, "I went to Red Hook High."

"I went to F.D.R. High in Hyde Park," Missy said.

Jana tried again. "Missy loves children. Do you like children, Jason?"

"I love them," Jason said.

Missy perked up. "Me too. B.J. says the cutest things. And he's so bright. He can already read his letters and say his numbers up to fifty. He recites his prayers and knows his fairytales."

Jason breathed a sigh of relief. "That's terrific. My little cousin is like that. She can sing Broadway show tunes."

Jana stepped out from between them.

"That's amazing," Missy said to Jason with a smile.

Jason beamed like snow under a headlight. "Do you want to be a teacher someday, Missy?"

"I like being a nanny. It lets me really enjoy kids one on one."

"That's terrific. And I can see you're really good at it."

Missy blushed. "Thank you, Jason. That's very sweet of you."

"It's the truth." Jason continued. "Someday I want

to have a pack of kids of my own."

She laughed. "You'll need a wife to help."

"I guess I will." He returned the laugh. "Do you want to have kids, too, Missy?"

She nodded. "I can't think of anything better than living in a house full of kids." Suddenly Missy's eyes filled with moisture. "I better go get B.J. Excuse me." She hurried off.

Jason's face drooped. "Did I say something wrong?"

"No, you didn't." Jana held his arm. "Missy is going through a rough time."

"I'm sorry to hear that. Is there anything I can do to help?"

"Don't give up on her." Jana walked over to Herm and Karen.

Herm, wearing a flannel shirt and jeans, rose. "Know your lines?"

Ever since I was five years old. "I'm looking forward to today's scenes."

Karen stood in a scarlet bodice blouse, tight black leather skirt, and pop finger leather gloves with a large skullcap ring on her middle finger. "Unfortunately, I don't have any lines—or scenes. I was just telling Herm how differently I would play Christa's role on this episode."

Herm bit at the skin where he once had fingernails. "Karen has some great ideas."

Bove returned with B.J., and they sat next to Simon on a sofa.

Jana smiled. "I'm sure more roles will come your way, Karen."

"Tell that to Bove"—Karen grimaced at Bove and

Simon—"and his new agent." She turned to Jana. "I guess I should direct that to you. Are you and my soon-to-be ex having fun in your mansion with your hubby away?"

Count to ten. "Bove is staying in my guest cottage."

"That's the party line." Karen smiled at Herm who picked at a pockmark.

Jana couldn't resist. "Karen, would you like some advice from an old hand at acting?"

"Sure."

"People in show business are…people. We work hard for a good product. We support one another in good times and bad. And we like working with other people who share those same ideals."

Karen patted at her stiff blonde hair. "Simon believed in you at six years old. Stu did the same for Christa when she was twenty-five. I'm thirty, Jana. Who's in line to help *me*?"

A production assistant with a squawking walkie-talkie asked Jana, Bove, and B.J. to follow her to the room set up as Jana's hospital room. When they got there, the crew finished shooting a scene where Nick follows Christa down the hallway. Again, only Nick's arm was visible to the camera in order to keep the identity of the killer a secret.

Once Jana was lying under the sheet in her hospital gown, Bove and B.J. stood next to the bed. She couldn't help imagining the same scenario if her fears were confirmed about the lump in her breast. Would Brian, Devon, Ed, and B.J. be relegated to frequent hospital visitors? Would she be able to take care of her children, make love to her husband, act in more episodes of her new television show? *Put it out of your mind, girl. Concentrate on the scene.*

They rehearsed the scene, where Jana tells her husband something is amiss at the hospital, and he dismisses her concerns as delusions from the anesthesia. Since Jana told Brian about her suspicions of murder a number of times in the past, she used emotional recall to make the scene realistic. She loved acting the dichotomy of enjoying the visit with her family, her concern for her nurse Christa, and fearing there was something very wrong at the hospital. Bove seemed to have no problem acting his concern for her. He added in a goodbye kiss on the cheek. *I don't mind.* B.J. ad libbed his exit line, "Since Mommy's better, Clownie can come home with me." *My son, the author.*

They shot the scene on the three of them, then did close-ups. The crew applauded at the last take. The lighting head asked for a break to replace a broken light. B.J. took Bove's hand. "You're a good dad."

Bove grinned. "And you're a good son."

Jana took B.J.'s other hand. "Bove is your pretend dad, and he's my make-believe husband."

"I like play pretend," B.J. answered.

"Me, too." Bove winked at her.

Jana asked Missy to take B.J. to the meeting room to play.

Sitting at the edge of her bed, Bove said to Jana, "B.J.'s a great kid."

"He's sure taken with you."

"He misses his father."

"Thanks for picking up the slack."

"Any time." Bove smiled. "I had a nice time last night."

Jana replied, "Me too."

"Jana Lane is the best girl I've ever dated."

"And the only one who didn't break your heart."

"Not true."

She squeezed his strong hand.

He whispered in her ear, "I talked to Nick."

"And?"

"Uncle Nick doesn't like his nephew-in-law."

"How come?"

"They see Christa's career as going in different directions."

Jana nodded. "Nick sees himself in the picture." *No pun intended.* "And Andrew doesn't. Andrew thinks having Nick at Christa's coattails will weigh her down."

Bove patted her leg over the sheet. "Good girl."

Simon giggled. "I'd say, 'Go get a room you two,' but you already have one!"

"Simon!" Jana couldn't help smiling.

From the other side of her bed, Simon, wearing a tangelo and vermillion jumpsuit, pinched her cheek. "My three clients were wonderful in that scene." He adjusted his honey-colored scarf. "What a beautiful family. And so convincing, I wonder if life will imitate art."

Bove said, "Sounds like a good concept to me."

Ignoring Bove, Jana turned to Simon. "Speaking of real life, are you working on what we talked about over the phone?"

Simon's dark eyes rose to the boom mic. "Cornelius and I have been slaving away like children in a sweatshop in Honduras. The Jana Lane AIDS Foundation will launch like the space shuttle Atlantis, starting with your first interview this afternoon. Harriet Hologram is coming to the set with her camera crew to interview you."

Bove whistled. "You must be important."

"You'll be featured on her television show tonight," Simon said proudly.

"Thank you, Simon." Jana squeezed his arm.

"Don't thank me, baby doll. Just give that old bloodhound a good interview."

"I will."

Herm barked away Bove and Simon, and shot a scene with the camera on a dolly following Jana from office to office as she searched through desk drawers, filing cabinets, phone messages, and listened at doorways in an attempt to uncover who was behind the illegal selling of patient organs and the night nurse's murder. As Jana raced from room to room with the camera at her heels, she was thankful for all her home workout sessions. She was also thankful for Jason Franks and all of his props. Running in the hospital hallway, she experienced flashbacks from her nightmares. Jana focused on her role and pushed the disturbing images out of her mind.

When Herm was satisfied with the shots, a production assistant led Jana back to her hospital room. *Having not gotten much sleep last night, I can use the rest.* With her head on the pillow, despite the squawking from the walkie-talkie and the pandemonium of people and equipment around her, Jana nearly nodded off. She revived when Alaster, Siobhan, Hyo, and Aisha joined her, and Herm talked them all through the mechanics of the next scene. Art imitated life as every time Jana tried to drift off to sleep, a hospital worker entered her room and disturbed her. Following directions from the real nurse, Hyo, as the orderly, brought Jana milk and broth. Siobhan, as another day nurse, took Jana's vitals. Alaster and Aisha, as doctor and intern, listened to her heart, checked her reflexes, and asked questions about her health. When the others left, Jana asked Alaster about what Christa had told her the evening before. Alaster dropped a few clues about seeing the hospital administrator talking to some shady types in his office, and his surprise about Nick's rise from paper pusher to head hospital administrator practically overnight. As they rehearsed the scene, Jana couldn't help notice the furtive glances between the two couples. *What secret are they hiding?*

Herm did the long shot, then Jana's close-up. Though only at the beginning of their careers, the four young people impressed Jana with the competence and believability of their performances. She wondered if they had actually worked at a hospital, given their ease and efficiency with the equipment and medical jargon.

Herm called, "Cut!"

As the technicians raced around to set up for the next shot, Herm told the actors to take a lunch break. Jana rose from the bed and put on her robe. "Nice job."

"Thank you," Alaster replied. "That means a lot coming from you."

His girlfriend Siobhan added, "We're thrilled to be working with you, Jana."

Aisha and Hyo grinned at each other. Aisha said, "You're a real pro, Jana."

Hyo added, "Unlike *some* people on set."

Aisha gave her boyfriend a silencing glance.

That's my cue. "Would you four like to join me for

lunch in the solarium upstairs?"

The couples looked at one another as if being asked to the principal's office.

"I promise I won't bite." Jana smiled.

Aisha spoke first. "We're honored that you asked us."

Sibohan piped up next. "But we don't want to bother you."

A bit wooden for such a good actor, Hyo said, "I'm sure you have more important things to do than eat with *us*."

Jana replied, "What's more important than lunch?"

"How about your son?" Alaster asked, clearly searching for a way out of eating with Jana.

"I asked his nanny to watch him. Please, won't you join me?"

Looking like teenagers who had just come down with hives, the four of them replied in unison, "We'd love to."

A few minutes later, Jana sat in the old hospital's all-glass circular solarium at the head of a round wooden table with one couple at her left and the other toward her right. The sun shone through the windows bathing them in a rainbow of indigo, gold, peach, and magenta. The actors brought salads from the salad bar in the main room along with bottled water.

Jana tasted her spinach salad with roasted beets, asparagus, cauliflower, and a honey yogurt dressing. "After all these years, I've never figured out why food on sets always tastes better than meals at home."

Aisha flicked back her long dark hair. "Probably because we don't have to make it."

Hyo wrapped his arm around his girlfriend. "I'm

sure Jana doesn't cook, Aisha."

Jana nearly spit out her water. "I cook all the time. I enjoy it."

"That's because you don't *have* to do it." Siobhan blinked her shamrock-colored eyes.

"Is that why you four have been so evasive with me?" Jana asked.

Alaster ran a hand through his blond locks. "What do you mean, Jana?"

Jana placed her fork on the table. "May I be honest with you?"

They all nodded like kids being asked if they'd like to stay up past their bedtime.

"I know you four are hiding something, and I'm well aware it involves Christa Bianca in some way. I also believe you think you will get in trouble if others find out the truth—including me."

The two couples looked down at their food like prison inmates facing the warden.

Jana said, "You don't know me. And you have no reason to trust me. All I can give you is my word that I want to help you. And I hope that's enough. Because I can't give you anything else."

Hyo said, "I trust you, Jana."

Alaster nodded. "So do I."

"And we've been telling Aisha and Siobhan that we can confide in you," Alaster added.

The two young women slumped down in their seats.

Jana said to the women, "I want to help you, but I can't do that unless you level with me. What's going on?"

Alaster looked at the other three. When they finally

nodded, he said, "Christa and Andrew got here early yesterday. And so did we."

Hyo added, "But we didn't know anyone else was here."

Siobhan explained, "Aisha was feeling tense about starting the new shoot."

Jana laughed. "I've been doing this since I was six years old, and I still get butterflies the first day of shooting. What's wrong with that?"

Aisha and Siobhan shared a worried glance. Finally Aisha said, "When I get nervous, I like to be comforted."

"Who doesn't?" Jana replied.

"Hyo was feeling the same way as Aisha," Alaster explained.

"And that's when Christa and Andrew saw us," Hyo said.

Jana felt as if she didn't speak the language. "Christa and Andrew saw Hyo and Aisha comforting one another?"

"Not exactly." Alaster blushed. "They saw me hugging Hyo.

"And Aisha's head on my shoulder," Siobhan added with a glance at Aisha.

As if a spotlight was turned on, Jana said, "Because Hyo and Alaster are a couple, and Aisha and Siobhan are a couple."

They nodded.

Jana continued. "And since the four of you are friends, you tell people the couples are Hyo and Aisha, and Alaster and Siobhan." *And I with my gay best friend and gay agent didn't see this!*

Siobhan explained, "Aisha and I met and fell in

love in college."

"Alaster and I did the same," Hyo added.

"We were all theater majors," Aisha said. "I got cast as Hyo's girlfriend in a show."

"And I was cast as Siobhan's boyfriend in the same show," Alaster explained.

Siobhan said, "Since we all wanted to be professional actors, we decided to extend the role play into real life."

Jana asked, "But why?"

Alaster's smooth face seemed to age ten years. "The sodomy laws are still on the books in some states."

"But anyone can be guilty of sodomy," Jana said.

"But only gay people are prosecuted," Alaster replied.

Jana said, "Thankfully that archaic law is off the books in New York and California. And the federal case is heading to the Supreme Court, where it is expected to be overturned."

Aisha said, "But it is still totally legal to fire someone for being gay, including in New York!"

Siobhan added, "And it's even worse in show business. The older generation of actors are so entrenched in the closet they smell like mothballs. Agents tell their young clients to stay hidden. Casting directors won't recommend openly gay actors. Producers and network executives blacklist them."

"But many of the people you mentioned are often gay themselves," Jana said.

"And they're the worst." Hyo rubbed his forehead. "It's like in the military. Guilt by association. Agents, casting directors, and producers don't want to be found out and lose their jobs, so they blow the whistle on others."

"And they force the screenwriters to change the gay characters to straight as they did in *Cat on a Hot Tin Roof* or just this year in *The Color Purple*," Aisha said.

Jana felt as if she had entered a House of Horrors. "What about William Hurt in *Kiss of the Spider Woman*?"

Alaster explained, "Hurt is straight, and his character dies at the end of the movie. So they let that one slip by."

"But surely things are changing," Jana said.

"They are," Alaster said.

"For the worse," Hyo added. "Thanks to conservative politicians and tax-exempt megachurch leaders, AIDS and gay now mean the same thing. Nobody wants to see that on the screen."

Christa and Andrew come from a small, rural town. Christa told Missy AIDS is God's punishment. "And Christa reacted negatively when she walked in on you four."

Siobhan said with her beautiful face full of love, "I had my arm around Aisha, and her head was on my shoulder. I kissed her cheek and told her everything would be okay."

Alaster smiled at Hyo. "I was doing the same with Hyo, but everything was definitely *not* okay."

"What did Christa say to you?" Jana asked, bracing herself for their reply.

They looked at one another, then Aisha acted as spokesperson. "Christa asked us why we chose our 'deviant lifestyle.'"

"I wanted to ask her when she chose to be straight, but I chickened out," Hyo said.

Aisha continued. "Christa said what we were doing was unnatural and against the Bible."

"So is wearing makeup, but Christa was doing *that*," Jana said.

"Andrew asked us if we knew homosexuals are all going to Hell," Hyo said. "We've heard these things before at church, on television, and from one of the political parties."

"It hurts each time," Alaster explained.

Jana said, "It's despicable fearmongering and bullying."

Alaster said, "But what frightened us the most was the fear of being fired."

Aisha said, "Like most actors who aren't stars, we work sporadically when the jobs come.

It's not so different for stars.

Siobhan clutched at her napkin as if it was worry beads. "Since Christa is the featured guest star of the pilot episode, we keep waiting for the ax to fall on the four of us."

Jana looked at them like a mother addressing children who are afraid of the dark. "Thank you for sharing this with me. You have my word it will go no farther than this table."

The four of them breathed a sigh of relief.

"You also have my word as the star and as a producer on this show, *none* of you will be fired."

Tears filled Aisha's dark eyes. "Thank you, Jana."

Siobhan took her girlfriend's hand. "We owe you big time, Jana."

"You don't owe me anything." Jana smiled. "Like

everyone else on the planet, you have the right to love whomever you love, and work without fear of discrimination and bullying."

Hyo wrapped his arm around Alaster. Alaster said to the two women, "I told you we could trust her."

"Alaster and I told the women about your AIDS fundraisers," Hyo said.

My fundraisers! "How would you four like a long-term acting job?"

They looked at one another as if Christmas had come early.

Jana explained, "Since our president and Congress continue to turn a deaf ear to the AIDS crisis, I am starting a new foundation to raise money for research, treatment, and care. I am going to send performers out on the road to entertain and raise money all over the US. You four impressed me today at the shoot. Are you interested?"

"Alaster and Hyo are amazing singers," Aisha said.

"And Aisha and I can cut up a rug as dancers," Siobhan added.

"And you are all strong actors, as you proved today," Jana said. "Do we have a deal?"

Tears streamed down their faces as they hugged and kissed one another. Finally Alaster turned to Jana. "Can I hug you?"

"I'll take back the job offer if you don't."

The four of them huddled around Jana, and they shared a group hug.

They finished their lunches then headed downstairs to the main meeting room. Jana knew where to find Simon—at the food table. She looked down at his full plate. "Enjoying lunch?"

Simon tugged at his girdle. "At my age, one needs to keep up his strength."

Jana couldn't resist. "Exactly how old *are* you, Simon?"

"I'm so old my social security number is 1, baby doll." Simon giggled. "But Cornelius helped me *rise* from the dead."

She patted his arm playfully. "You always make me smile, Simon."

"Good. Harriet Hologram will be here shortly."

Jana looked over at Alaster, Hyo, Aisha, and Siobhan sitting together in a corner of the room. "While I change clothes, I have something I need you to do for me."

He bowed. "Your wish is my command." His face hardened. "As long as it doesn't entail speaking with Christa and Andrew Bianca."

Jana did a double-take. "What do you have against *them*?"

"Nothing. But they clearly have something against *me*."

"Care to explain?"

Simon pursed his lips. "I ate lunch with them. Andrew made a comment about my jumpsuit being 'a tad flamboyant.'"

That's putting it mildly.

He adjusted his chartreuse waist pouch. "Christa laughed and said, 'You better be careful, Simon. People might think you're a homosexual.' When I said that I am indeed gay, Christa said she would pray for me to change. I asked, 'Change into what?' Andrew said it is God's will that I marry. I said I would in fact marry Cornelius, but it's against the law. Andrew said

Cornelius and I are against *God's* law. Then Christa said God wants me to procreate. I replied, 'At my age!'"

Jana couldn't help laughing.

"I'm glad you find this funny, baby girl."

"Simon, it's not funny. It's ridiculous. As are all forms of prejudice."

"Thank you, baby doll." Simon adjusted his silk scarf.

"Don't thank me, Simon. Do something for me. Do you see the two couples over there?"

Simon glanced over at Hyo, Alaster, Aisha, and Siobhan. "You mean the two gay couples?"

Jana's jaw dropped. "You could tell?"

"Someone in a coma could tell."

"*I* couldn't."

He smiled. "That's what makes you such a great actress—your ingenuousness."

"Thanks." *I think.* "Have you started preparations for the fundraising tour for AIDS?"

He nodded. "I hired a booking manager, public relations director, producer, director, writer, costumer, set designer, and road manager." Simon grinned like the Cheshire Cat. "With your money."

"Have you hired the performers yet?"

"Not yet."

"You've hired four today. I'd like you to use Hyo, Alaster, Aisha, and Siobhan. Can you please speak to them about it, and prepare their contracts?"

"Let me welcome Harriet first and bring her to the terrace." Simon rested his plate, no doubt his third or fourth, on the buffet table. "I hope I don't wither away from starvation."

Jana said to his small back, "Thank you, Simon." Jana checked in on B.J. and Missy, playing a card game on a sofa with Jason Franks. As earlier, Jason seemed to be perusing the room, in particular Christa, Andrew, and Nick who were eating their lunch on a nearby sofa. Jana also noticed Herm and Karen with their heads together in a private corner, and Bove brooding by the window.

"Who's winning?" Jana asked.

"Clownie!" B.J. replied, kissing his rag doll.

"Did you enjoy your lunch?"

"I like pastrami!" B.J. replied to his mother.

Jana explained to Jason, "A habit B.J. picked up when we did a play in New York City."

Jason asked, "Did you live in New York City, Missy?"

Missy shook her head. "That was before I became B.J.'s nanny."

"Then B.J. didn't have the best nanny yet," Jason said with smile.

Missy blushed. "And Jana didn't have the best prop master yet."

They shared an enamored gaze.

"I like Missy and Jason," B.J. said to his mom.

"I like them, too," Jana replied. *And they clearly like each other.*

Jana kissed the top of her son's head, then blinked back tears. *I may not be around to watch him grow.* Jana made her way to her dressing room, where she changed back into her pink and white pants suit and gold leaf jewelry. The tears filled her eyes. She tried to blink them back again, but more tears came. Before she knew it, Jana was bent over, sobbing in hysterics. *Pull yourself together, girl. You'll see Dr. Borress tomorrow.* Jana took in some deep breaths. She quickly wiped her eyes with a tissue, repaired her makeup, then hurried to the outdoor terrace toward the rear of the old hospital, where Harriet Hologram and her staff were waiting.

Harriet Hologram, looking eighty going on a hundred and ten, extended a wrinkled, manicured, and bejeweled hand. "Jana, my dear, how are you?"

Jana smiled at the familiar stiff blonde wig, heavy makeup, and slit eyes no doubt from too many facelifts. "It's nice to see you again, Harriet. Thank you for coming from New York City."

"I'd travel anywhere for an interview with Jana Lane." Jana felt a bony elbow in her side. "We legends have to stick together." Harriet motioned for Jana to sit on an overstuffed rose-colored easy chair across from a similar chair at the foot of the balcony. "The view of the sky, mountains, trees, and lawn are so beautiful from up here. Just like Jana Lane."

A heavyset makeup woman touched up their hair and makeup as Harriet's sound operator wired them with lavalier microphones. The camera operator turned on the lights and camera. "Ready when you are, Harriet."

With a gold lace dress and gold jewelry hanging off her rail-thin body, Harriet sat across from Jana and offered her a denture-laden smile. "You are just as adorable as when I first interviewed you in LA when you were six years old. Do you remember that?"

You asked me if my mother spanked me, and if my father was jealous of my success. "I sure do."

Harriet, clearly not an actress, pretended not to

remember. "How many times have I interviewed you, Jana?"

"Six."

"And every one a gem!"

And a nightmare.

"I'm featuring this interview on my show tonight. Jana Lane is always big news."

For your big claws.

The audio operator had them do a sound check. When Harriet nodded, the camera rolled. Harriet smiled into the camera. "I am here today on the set of Jana Lane's new network television mystery series, *The Detective's Wife*. Watch."

Jana looked at a television monitor set up on the balcony. She watched a segment Harriet had obviously shot while Jana was having lunch with the two couples. It was the typical short edited segment showing some of the set locations, a brief interview with Herm proclaiming the merits of the pilot, a quick interview with Bove speaking about his transition from professional football player to detective to actor, and a short interview with Christa discussing her rise to fame from the Flaming Foliage Festival Queen to starring in the indie hit *On My Own*.

With the camera back on Harriet, the entertainment news reporter smiled at Jana. "Jana Lane, what a career you had. Your father put you in his movies when you were a child and a teen. We heard nothing from you for twenty years. Then you resurfaced out of nowhere as a has-been starring in two films and a Broadway play enjoyed by the few nostalgia fans who still remembered you from the old days. And weren't the Oscar and Tony Award voters kind to give you those awards?" She offered a smug look to the camera. "As if to say, 'The world may have forgotten, but we still remember your old glory days from an era long gone.'"

Jana squirmed in her chair.

Harriet continued her performance. "And now a married mother of three, when the big screen has faded to black for you, television has come to the rescue with a series—that you yourself are producing." Harriet sighed as if sitting at the bedside of a terminally ill patient. "Welcome back, Jana."

"Thank you, Harriet." Jana smiled at the camera. "Nevgere Productions has created quite an interesting show, and I'm thrilled to be a part of it."

Harriet looked as if she had tasted sour milk and rotten eggs. "I read the pilot script, and it seems you spend most of it in bed. Was that decision made due to your advanced age?"

Keep it up, Harriet, and I'll ask yours. "It's a thrilling story about a detective's wife who enters the hospital with appendicitis and uncovers a shocking secret going on behind closed doors at the hospital."

"Andrew Bianca told me his wife carries most of the episode as the head nurse who is in peril from someone at the hospital. Don't worry, Jana. I'm sworn to secrecy about the identity of the murderer. He or she will no doubt carry the show's heavy-weight acting at the final confession scene."

"I hope everyone tunes in." Jana looked at the camera. "You won't be disappointed by this fast-paced, white knuckled, entertaining mystery."

"And if the show doesn't catch on, what's next for you, Jana? Doing *Hello, Dolly* at a dinner theatre in the Midwest?"

Jana smiled at the camera. "With all the terrific talent around me, I'm pretty confident this show will run for years."

"The viewers will be the judge of that," Harriet said as if speaking about a child's stick figure drawing. "And I understand you are planning to start a new little project."

Jana slid to the edge of her seat. "With my agent's help, I am in the process of putting together the Jana Lane AIDS Foundation to raise much needed money for the research, treatment, and care of people with AIDS."

Harriet grimaced. "Isn't AIDS a taboo topic in Hollywood? You seem to be the only celebrity taking up the gauntlet. Is it an attempt at getting some press?"

"Sadly, our elected officials, and as you say the leaders of our industry, like most people have shunned the victims of this dreaded disease that has claimed the lives of so many. We desperately need funds and manpower."

"And you weren't able to achieve that with your three little fundraisers in the past?"

"I thank all of the entertainers who so generously devoted their time and talents, but the money we raised barely put a dent in what is needed to fight this plague. My plan is to send out troops of performers in variety road shows touring all over the US to entertain and raise money, as was done during World War II with the USO shows. Today I am declaring a war on AIDS."

Harriet's lipstick cracked. "And what do you say to the many people who share *this* point of view?" She gestured toward the monitor.

Christa's large eyes over her honeysuckle dress filled the screen. "My religion teaches AIDS is God's wrath against sin."

Andrew was next with a look that drooped off his face like his large glasses and old suit. "My pastor taught me that if you want to dance you have to pay the fiddler. If these homosexuals want to do…whatever they do…God won't sit idly by."

"Jana?" Harriet, and the camera, pointed at Jana.

"I don't believe hurricanes, earthquakes, and diseases are God's wrath against us. My religion teaches me to help those in need, not disparage and demonize them."

Harriet quickly switched gears with, "You had some pretty racy love scenes with your leading men in *His Obsession*, *Madame Senator*, and *China Doll*. Now hunky Chris Bove plays your husband in this series. How does your real life husband feel about this?"

Thankfully he isn't here to answer. "Brian understands make-believe is a part of the work day for an actress."

"I didn't see your husband on set."

"He's in Florida designing new malls."

"I see." Harriet grinned as if laying down a winning hand at a card game, and pointed to the monitor. Karen Evans appeared on screen. "Bove and I had a strong marriage. Bove met Jana Lane."

Bove appeared looking amazing in a tight polo shirt that matched his eyes. "Jana is the most captivating woman I have ever known. It's easy to play her husband in the show. I adore her. We have a past. I'm staying with her during the shoot."

Simon was next. "My baby doll and Bove make an incredible couple."

B.J. was last. "Bove's my new dad!"

Harriet gloated. "May I break the story of your divorce, Jana?"

There may be real murders committed on this set— by me. Jana looked deeply into the camera. "In my old movie, *The Littlest Farmer*, the other children in the village told me they saw little Timmy with stolen eggs from my family's barn. When I told my father about it, he gave me good advice that I still live by today. 'If you want to find out the truth, always go to the source.' When I confronted Timmy about the lost eggs, I found out that Timmy had in fact caught the egg thief and was returning my family's eggs." She smiled. "Only *I* know the truth about my personal life, and I can assure everyone watching that my love and devotion for my husband, and his for me, are as strong as ever. While Chris Bove is an enticing and captivating partner, our union is solely on screen."

Harriet turned toward the camera. "I have the feeling this is a story to be continued. Let's keep an eye on Jana Lane to see if the show is cancelled, her marriage cracks, and she ventures into Chris Bove's egg basket."

The lights went off. Harriet threw her scaly arms around Jana. "Thank you for the wonderful interview, Jana. The ratings for both of our shows will shoot through the roof." She kissed Jana's cheek. "Give your handsome husband a hug for me. Until next time!"

The technicians offered Jana an apologetic look, then followed Harriet out of the room.

Like a bull headed for the ring, Jana stormed through the hospital corridors and entered the main meeting room. She pushed Bove's shoulder like a street fighter challenging the champ. "'Jana is the most captivating woman I have ever known. It's easy to play her husband in the show. I adore her. We have a past. I'm staying with her during the shoot.' Why did you say those things to Harriet Hologram?"

Bove's strong jaw dropped. "I didn't say that."

"Then somebody must be a terrific ventriloquist, because I saw you on tape, Bove."

He ran a hand through his thick hair. "I said it, but not in that way."

"In what way did you say it?"

He sighed. "When Harriet interviewed me I said each of those phrases, but not joined together like that. I said a lot of other things in between them."

And Harriet edited it so you would say what she wanted you to say. "And I'm guessing Karen didn't say you had a strong marriage until I came along."

He laughed. "No way. Karen said our marriage was strong in the beginning. About five minutes later in the interview, she said I met you in DC during *Madame Senator*."

Jana felt her blood pressure lower. "I'm sorry, Bove."

"Did you really think I would say something to the press that might reflect badly on you?" His eyes were wide and questioning.

"I wasn't thinking clearly."

"Obviously." He pouted.

"What can I do to make it up to you?"

"Make me dinner tonight."

"No way. You'll spend the whole meal telling me I didn't use enough garlic, or that I should import my parsley from Brazil."

He smiled. "All right, come to the cottage tonight

at seven for dinner."

"What are you making?"

He whispered in her ear, "Something mouthwatering."

As his shoulder rubbed against hers, the scent of pine filled the air. Jana couldn't help swooning a bit.

Bove seemed to notice. "Can I trust you to behave alone with me?"

"I'll do my best."

B.J. ran into Bove's arms. "Can I have dinner with you, too?"

Before Bove could reply, Jana said, "Not tonight, B.J."

A production assistant called for Jana. Bove played catch with B.J., and Jana followed the squawking walkie-talkie to the wardrobe room then changed back into her hospital patient garb in her dressing room.

As Jana entered one of the rooms set up as an office, Nicholas Hartford, in his three-piece suit, sat behind the desk with the overhead lighting causing his gray hair to shine. Jana took her seat across from the desk. Herm stood over them while they rehearsed the scene where Jana fabricates a displeasure with the hospital in order to confront Nick with her suspicions about his illegal activities. *Why is Nick using his script?* The rehearsal went fine with Nick and Jana playing a cat and mouse game, where he evades her questions and she continues to try to trap a rat—and a murderer. Jana enjoyed sparring with the seasoned actor, and he seemed to relish being back before the camera. The scene ended with Jana accidentally mentioning her snooping and Christa's suspicions of Nick.

Herm called for the slate, and Nick hid his script in

the top desk drawer.

"Rolling, slate, action!"

Jana said her first line and waited. Fear crept into Nick's face.

Herm called, "Cut!" He picked at the pockmarks on his chin. "What's wrong?"

Nick replied, "I went up on my lines. It won't happen again."

"All right. Roll, take two, action!"

Again Jana said her first line. "Thank you for meeting with me."

Again nothing from Nick.

Jana ad libbed a line to help Nick remember his line. "I'm sure you are very busy, but it's imperative that I speak with you."

Nick's vacant stare led to Herm shouting, "Cut!"

"I knew the lines last night," Nick said.

"This isn't last night." Herm bit at the skin at his cuticles. "You need to know them *now*."

"I will. I do. Give me one more take," Nick said like a prisoner asking for parole.

"Roll, take three, action!"

"Thank you for meeting me," Jana said, remembering the illusion of the first time—saying each line as if it were the first time she was saying it, regardless of how many takes were required.

When nothing came out of Nick's mouth but hot air, Herm called, "Cut!"

Seeing Herm's red face, Jana said, "My father had the same problem on my last film with him, *Sugar and Spice*. He played the sheriff. For the scenes in his office, he hid the script on his desk blotter and glanced down when he needed it. Let's try my dad's technique.

How about it, Nick?"

"Is that all right, Herm?"

Herm shouted at Nick, "Whatever will get this scene shot!"

Nick took the two pages for the scene out of his script and placed them on the desk blotter. Jana moved the desk clock between the papers and the camera. *Thanks, Jason.*

"Camera, take four, action!"

They shot the scene as the two-shot. Since Nick's performance was uninspired, Jana tried to fill in the gaps with as many nonverbal reactions as she could without rivaling Harpo Marx.

Nick was able to use his script for the close-up on Jana. For Nick's close-up, a production assistant held Nick's pages next to the camera, and he read his lines like a novice local newscaster.

When the scene was finally over, Herm called out, "Cut!" with a look of relief on his lined face.

Nick said, "I'm just a bit rusty. I'll be better in my next scene."

Herm swallowed two aspirin and barked out orders to the technicians.

Andrew Bianca came forward from the crowd of onlookers. "That was pathetic, Nick. Christa got you this job because you're her uncle. But the gravy train stops here."

Nick put his arm around his nephew-in-law. "Maybe Christa and I will get a spin-off series. Look at *Cocoon*. Older actors are in again."

Andrew replied, "Older actors who can still cut it, that is. Christa doesn't need an ancient albatross around her neck."

So much for respecting your elders. Jana rose. "Andrew, Nick did his best. We made it work."

Andrew turned to Jana like a pit bull facing a kitten. "Nothing works for me except seeing Christa's star rise, and nobody, including her daffy uncle, will shoot her star down." He stormed off.

Jana patted Nick's shoulder and told a white lie. "The scene went fine, Nick."

Choked up from Andrew's tirade, Nick said, "Excuse me." And he walked out of the room.

While the crew set up for the next scene, Jana followed Andrew to the main meeting room. She found B.J. on Bove's lap with Bove reading him a story and Missy napping next to them on the sofa. Jana looked over at the far corner of the room and found Nick in what appeared to be a heated exchange with Hyo. She walked over to them. "Is there a problem?"

Nick unveiled a fabricated smile. "I was just giving a bit of advice to the youngster."

Hyo glared at Nick. "But unfortunately Nick wasn't listening to *my* advice."

"Which is?"

"A difference in acting techniques," Nick replied to Jana. "I'm old school presentational style, and young Hyo here is strictly representational method."

"Go ahead. Tell Jana about your presentational style, Nick." Hyo scowled at Nick then joined Alaster on a loveseat, sitting opposite Aisha and Siobhan.

Jana turned to Nick. "Why was he so angry?"

"You know young people. Rebels without causes. Will you excuse me?" Nick hurried out of the room.

Jana joined Andrew and Christa standing beside an old brick fireplace. "Don't you think you were a little hard on Nick?" Jana asked Andrew.

Christa held Andrew's arm. "What did you say to Uncle Nick, honey?"

Jana explained, "Nick had some line problems in our scene."

"Yeah, he couldn't remember any of them," Andrew said.

"Many actors forget their lines." *Except for B.J.*

"The guy should hang it up, before he hangs up Christa's career," Andrew said through his nose.

Christa took Andrew's hands. "Honey, I know Uncle Nick has his problems, but he was my idol growing up. With my brother and sisters busy with their own lives, Uncle Nick is the only family I have near me. Except for you. Please try to understand."

They kissed.

"All right." Andrew added, "So long as he knows that with Stu gone *I'm* the one running your career."

Christa rested her head on Andrew's shoulder. "Everyone knows you're my main man, and I wouldn't want it any other way."

He kissed her forehead. "I want to talk to Herm about your next scene. Will you be all right here?"

"Of course." Christa squeezed Jana's hand. "Jana Lane, the girl who saved her friend Timmy from sharks, volcanoes, earthquakes, bandits, and gorillas, is with me."

Jana laughed. "Do they have those in closed hospitals?"

Andrew narrowed his eyes at Jana. "Take care of my girl."

When they were alone, Jana said, "Christa, it's getting a bit claustrophobic in here. Neither of us is in the next scene. Let's go for a walk around the lake."

"I'd like that."

They changed back into their clothes then headed outside to a small lake with a stone bridge over it, surrounded by mountains in the distance. As they traversed the cobblestone walkway past emerald trees and the Kelly-green lawn, Jana enjoyed the golden rays of the sun bathing them under the clear blue sky.

Christa held Jana's hand. "Do you mind?"

"Not at all." Jana felt as if walking with the daughter she never had.

"This is such a beautiful spot. It reminds me of back home."

Jana said, "Tell me about it."

"Renovo was always a little lumber town tucked away in the mountains. It was so clean and beautiful. We lived in a log cabin my daddy built. My mama sewed the curtains, tablecloth, placemats, and our clothes. Like most of the men, Daddy worked in the lumber yard." Her beautiful face saddened. "But the thing about cutting down trees is you can get to the point where there's no trees left to cut. And the forest fires didn't help. Some nights I'd go to bed so hungry I wondered if I'd wake up the next morning. And the worst was seeing my little brother and sisters holding their stomachs. One time, I caught my little brother eating from a neighbor's garbage can. That just about broke my heart."

"You must have loved those visits from your uncle."

Christa giggled like a little girl. "Uncle Nick showed me there was a way out. Oh, how I wanted to leave with him and become an actor."

"And here you are."

They shared a smile.

Jana stopped at a bench and motioned for Christa to sit next to her. A robin red breast flew by them and landed in a tree branch overhead. Jana looked out at the lake. The silver ripples seemed to nuzzle against the surrounding rocks. "Christa, Missy said you told her AIDS is God's wrath. You and Andrew said that in Harriet Hologram's interview, too. You told Simon, Hyo, Alaster, Aisha, and Siobhan that being gay is immoral. Why did you do all that?"

"Because of the story of Sodom and Gomorrah."

"Which is about greed and rape. There are far more cautions about heterosexual sex than homosexual sex in the Bible."

"But the Old Testament says a man shall not lie with another man."

"And near that it forbids us to eat pork and wear clothing made of more than one fabric." *When all else fails, fight fire with fire.* "Do you remember the New Testament story about the Roman soldier asking Jesus to heal his sick slave?"

"Of course. We learned that in Sunday school."

"Have you ever asked yourself why a Roman soldier occupying Jerusalem would ask a Jewish rabbi to heal his servant?"

Christa shook her head no.

"Well, some people believe the common Greek translation is incorrect, and 'servant' should be 'lover.' If so, that sure changes the moral of the story."

Christa bit her lip. "But it's how I was raised."

"I was raised by a father who had no problem hurting anyone's feelings if it meant getting ahead in show business. I made a conscious choice to stray from that behavior." Jana asked, "Do you remember how you felt when the kids back home called you 'Rag Doll,' because you were so poor?"

She nodded. "I felt as if they were chipping away at my heart a little bit more each day."

"Because words hurt. And they can also take away our humanity. Do you really think calling other people names is Christ-like?"

Christa's eyes raced around in her head. "Jana, you've given me a great deal to think and pray about."

"I'm glad."

Christa hugged Jana. "I'm glad, too. I don't ever want to hurt or demean people the way the kids back in Renovo did to me."

"I'm so happy to hear you say that, Christa." Jana returned the hug then looked at her watch. "We better get back to the set before Herm gives Karen Evans both of our roles."

They shared a laugh as they walked back to the hospital, then changed into their hospital attire. Next, they followed a squawking walkie-talkie to a hallway in the hospital laden with lighting equipment, cameras, the boom microphone, and countless technicians.

Herm directed Jana to follow Nick down the hallway to a stairwell, then hide as Nick confronts Christa at the top of the landing. Though Nick was in the scene, he had no dialogue. Jana breathed a sigh of relief. Once Cindi freshened their makeup, Herm asked the assistant director to call for quiet. Jana noticed Simon, Hyo, Alaster, Aisha, Siobhan, Karen, and Missy watching.

Jana asked Missy, "Where's B.J.?"

Missy replied, "Bove took him outside for a walk. Is that all right?"

"Of course." Jana also noticed Andrew watching Nick like a store security guard staring at a kleptomaniac.

They rehearsed the scene with no mishaps, except for the camera getting stuck on the dolly. Once the technical problem was solved, Herm called for the camera, slate, and action. The camera followed Jana spying on Nick and Christa down the hallway and into the stairwell.

"Cut! Print!" Herm shouted, "Reload, reposition the camera and lighting, and we'll shoot the next scene right away. Position one, everybody."

Uh-oh. Nick has a great deal of dialogue in this scene. We may have to paste the script onto the stairwell. Jana took one look at Andrew and assumed he was thinking the same thing.

Pandemonium ensued as technicians scurried around like mice in a maze. Jana ducked when a piece of lighting equipment nearly grazed her head. Jason raced passed her carrying a fire extinguisher prop to the staircase. Nick stood at the top of the staircase looking like a rabbit facing a leaf blower. Christa blew a good luck kiss to him.

Suddenly Christa screamed. Jana peered through the sea of bodies and equipment, but Cindi covered her view. Jana raced to the stairwell, where she found Christa sobbing on the floor in Andrew's arms, and Nick's lifeless body at the bottom of the stairs.

Chapter 6

A half hour later, Jana was back in the lecture hall sitting on the fifth level between Bove and Simon. Bove put his arm around the back of her chair. She smelled pine as Bove asked, "What did you see?"

Jana's heart was still racing. Bove's bicep resting against her back didn't help. "Cindi."

"Cindi?"

"She walked in front of me just as Christa screamed."

"That's it? You're slipping *Girl Detective*."

"I was standing down the hallway, and Christa and Nick were on the stairwell."

"You must have seen *something* suspicious?"

Lieutenant Mario Rivera stood behind the podium wearing a dark suit and an even darker look on his face. As the day prior, Rivera scratched at his curly hair, sending a windstorm of white onto his shoulders. "May I have your attention please?" When the chatter ceased, Rivera cleared his throat. "I am sorry to report Nicholas Hartford suffered from a fall down the stairs, which killed him."

Sitting in the second row, Christa wept on Andrew's shoulder, and he patted her back. Jana also noticed Hyo, Alaster, Aisha, and Siobhan farther down her own row. *Is Hyo smiling?*

"We have taped off the area of the accident,"

Rivera explained.

Accident?

Rivera added, "My deputy and I have spoken with everyone near the scene. No one reported seeing anything out of the ordinary."

Bove whispered to Jana, "Except Nick plunging down the stairs."

"At least while falling, Nick didn't have any lines to remember—or forget," Simon said, followed by a slap on the shoulder from Jana.

"My intention was to close down this production for good." Rivera gestured to Herm sitting in the front row. "However, your director, and the producers I spoke with over the phone, asked me to reconsider. The compromise is that I am closing down production for one day while we further inspect and secure the premises. The following morning, I will post a police officer in the main meeting room and wherever you are shooting."

Herm stood and picked at a pockmark on his neck. "Since we're ahead of schedule, the show will be finished on time." Jana noticed him sit and take Karen's hand. She felt Bove's arm stiffen.

"Was there foul play, detective?" Cindi asked, sitting behind Jana.

"I am unable to comment on that at this time. However, you all can be assured, we will look into this and ensure your safety."

Bove whispered to Jana, "Like he's done so far?"

Once a detective, always a detective, Bove.

Rivera rubbed his neck, causing it to snow over the people sitting in the front row. "I ask that none of you speak to the press. Please stay in your hotel rooms and homes. Contact me if you remember anything or see anything out of the ordinary.

How about an incompetent local detective?

"My condolences to Mrs. Bianca and all of you for your loss."

Christa said to Andrew, "Why has the Lord forsaken me?"

Andrew kissed her forehead. "He hasn't. I'm here, baby."

Rivera concluded with, "Thank you all for your time. Please leave slowly and safely."

As everyone left the lecture hall, Jana and Bove met Cindi in the aisle. "Too bad you aren't a detective in real life, Bove."

Bove smiled. "I was."

"You were?" Cindi seemed more interested than ever.

"Back in DC."

"My sister lives in DC."

"Really, where?"

Jana excused herself and approached Christa at the front of the room. "I'm so sorry, Christa. What happened?"

Christa said between sobs, "We were…standing at the…top of the stairs. I…felt someone push me."

"Who?"

"It was…from behind. I…couldn't see."

Jana asked Andrew, "Did you see anyone?"

He shook his head then leveled his glasses onto his nose. "If I did, he would no longer be among the living."

Christa's tears sprayed onto her sundress and Jana's jacket. "I…started to fall…down the stairs, but

Andrew caught me. That must have been when Uncle Nick was pushed."

Jana asked, "Did you tell Lieutenant Rivera about the person who pushed you?"

Christa nodded. "He said nobody around me…saw anything."

Jana replied, "But there were so many people. *Somebody* had to see something!"

"Uncle Nick must have." Christa's eyes filled with tears as if suddenly realizing it. "But he's gone."

Andrew wrapped his arms around her. "It's okay, baby. I'll take care of you." He walked Christa to the door and out of the room.

Jana headed for Rivera.

"Mrs. Otley, your son is safe with your nanny. I told them to go home."

"I know where my son is, Detective. What I want to know is if you checked out my theory about Stu Silverman being poisoned. And why you told everyone a moment ago there was no foul play today when in reality Christa Bianca, and no doubt her uncle, were pushed?"

His dark eyes moved from side to side. "Please, follow me."

A few minutes later Jana sat next to Rivera in a room she surmised was once the hospital gift shop. Empty counters surrounded them as they sat on a window seat with the mountains reaching up to them.

"You were right, Mrs. Otley." Rivera read from a folder. "We found traces of oleander and hemlock on Mr. Silverman's lunch plate."

I knew it! "And you also know a falling light screen would have killed Christa Bianca yesterday had

Stu Silverman not saved her. And today someone tried unsuccessfully to push Christa down the stairs, but succeeded with Nick Hartford."

"I know all of that."

"Then why in the world did you tell everyone that you didn't suspect foul play?"

Rivera sighed. "The last thing I want to do is spread panic." He leaned back on the window seat. "Or tip off the murderer that I am investigating."

"So you admit there is a murderer on this set?"

"Unfortunately, I do." He raised his hands to the peeling ceiling. "But we have no fingerprints, no eye witnesses, and nobody caught with poison."

Jana rested her fists under chin. "There were so many people racing around Christa and Nick before he fell today."

"So it would be quite easy to miss someone giving Mrs. Bianca and her uncle a shove." He rose. "I will continue to question everyone in attendance. And I meant what I said about police officers stationed around the set when shooting resumes the day after tomorrow."

Jana stood and walked with Rivera to the door. "Thank you for confiding in me."

"As usual, I'm sure I didn't tell you anything you didn't already know." His eyes narrowed. "I'm not giving up until I catch whoever is doing this."

The car from the production company took Jana home. She phoned Devon and Ed with B.J. chattering next to her, then got B.J. his dinner, and tucked him— and Clownie—into bed. She sat on the rocking chair in front of the dancing bears and elephants on the wallpaper, and read him a story. Once she kissed him goodnight—five times, she left the bedroom and bumped into Missy.

"Does B.J. need anything?"

"He just fell asleep." Jana motioned for Missy to follow her down the hall. When they arrived at Missy's pumpkin-colored bedroom, they sat on the four-poster. "How are you doing?"

"I'm fine." Missy blinked back tears.

"Since we're off tomorrow, I'm going to work with Simon on the AIDS foundation."

"Good."

"How are you feeling?"

Missy moved her hair behind her ears. "A little tired."

"Did you tell your doctor?"

"He knows."

"If you have any other symptoms, please let me know."

Missy let the tears flow. "I can't believe you let me work for you."

"Missy, I know that Matty hurt you. And I understand why you're leery of trusting anyone. But there are people who care about you."

"Who?"

"Me...B.J....and Jason."

Her face lit up as if hit with a spotlight. "Do you really think Jason likes me?"

"I really do."

Missy sighed. "He won't when Christa blurts out that I have AIDS."

"Is that what you're worried about?"

Missy nodded.

Jana took Missy's hands. "Christa won't do that."

"Hah! I'm sure she can't wait."

131

"I spoke to her today. She may come around about some of her archaic ideas."

"She's acting." Missy walked to the balcony.

"I don't think so." Jana followed and looked out at the river hugging the mountains. "But I do think Jason should know about you."

Missy's tears inched down her cheeks. "Please don't tell him, Jana."

Grabbing her by the shoulders, Jana said, "I won't. But I think *you* should."

"Why would I do *that*?"

"Because you like him and he likes you. And when people like each other, they're honest with each other. Not only about the good things, but about the not so good things."

She shook her head. "He'll never understand. Jason won't speak to me again."

"Shouldn't you let Jason make that decision rather than making it for him?"

"Jason is the first friend I've made in a long while. What if after he finds out, he hates me?"

"Then he wasn't your friend." Jana put her arm around her. "Missy, why not give Jason the chance to prove his friendship to you?"

As Missy walked Jana to the door, she said, "I don't know what's going to happen with Jason, but I know I have one real friend. You."

Jana kissed her forehead. "Can you listen for B.J. while I'm at the cottage tonight?"

"Of course."

"You're a good nanny, Missy. And a good person. Have faith. You're going to be okay." *I should take my own advice.* Jana left the room and walked down the hallway.

When she got back to her bedroom, she answered the ringing French provincial phone and sat on her chaise.

"Remember me?"

"Brian, I can explain everything."

"You always can."

She took in a deep breath. "Harriet tricked Bove and his soon-to-be ex-wife, Karen. They said those things about me, but not in the way Harriet edited them."

"What are you talking about?"

"The interview I did on Harriet Hologram's television show tonight. Isn't that what *you're* talking about?"

"I don't watch crap like that—no offense."

None taken. "Then what are you talking about?"

"The TV news, which happened to report that an old character actor, Nicholas Hartford, fell down the stairs to his death on the set of *your* television show today."

"Oh, that." *Did I just sound British?*

"Yeah, that. On TV, Rivera said he thinks Hartford had a bad fall. But this is *your* production, Jan, so I know better. Who killed him? Is it the same person who killed Stu Silverman? Are you safe? Is our son out of harm's way?"

"Brian, please slow down."

He exhaled loudly. "All right. While I count to ten, tell me what is going on. And I hope the story ends with you and B.J. quitting the show."

Jana rested back on the gold-trimmed chaise and looked at her empty canopy bed. "B.J. and I are fine."

"But Stu Silverman and Nicholas Hartford clearly are not."

"The show is going well."

"Minus the two real murders."

"But—"

"Here it comes."

"—someone poisoned Stu and pushed Nick down the stairs. Whoever it was pushed Christa first, but Andrew saved her."

"Jan—"

"Anyone could have done it. As we know Rivera isn't the sharpest knife in the drawer. So I'm trying to figure out—"

"Jan!"

"What?"

"You love it, Jana Lane Otley."

"Of course I love acting."

"Not just acting. You love the thrill of the chase, and playing armchair detective. You thrive on it."

He's always known me better than I know myself. "Since you mention it. I get a thrill from acting, but after solving the other cases, I think I missed sleuthing. Trying to put together the pieces of the puzzle is really fun. It's like a drug. I miss it when I'm not on a case."

"On a case! You sound like a detective."

"Speaking of detectives, I'm having dinner with Bove."

"Of course!"

"To go over the suspects and clues."

"My own Holmes has a new Watson."

"And I have to admit, it is kind of exciting."

"Listen, Poirot, before you go off to sharpen the little gray cells, promise me you will protect the two greatest treasures I have—you and our son."

"Of course."

"And tell me you'll solve this soon."

"I will." *It's time to tell him.* "Brian, acting on the show and sleuthing have been good therapy for me."

"Therapy?"

"They've helped me to take my mind off something."

Panic filled his voice. "What is it, Jan?"

"Honey, I found a lump." She swallowed hard. "On my breast."

"I'm coming home."

"No, please don't, Brian. I'm seeing Dr. Borress tomorrow. It may be nothing to worry about." *But I'm worried.*

"Is it painful or red?"

"No."

"Do you feel sick?"

"I'm fine."

"Have you told anyone?"

"No."

"Why not?"

"I don't want to worry anyone, or watch their sad faces pitying me."

Brian asked, "Not even Simon?"

"Simon would have a heart attack."

"You shouldn't be going through this alone."

"I'm not. I'm talking to my wonderful husband. Besides, I don't know anything yet. It may be nothing serious."

"Let's hold onto that. Okay?"

"Okay." She could finally breathe.

"Call me the second you know anything."

"I will."

She heard a kiss through the phone.

"I adore you, Brian."

"You mean everything to me, babe. I'll be home in a week, unless you need me, then I'll be home in a few hours."

"Don't work too hard. No, work harder, and come home sooner."

"Act in your show. Think about your old movies, figure out who did it and why. And make sure Dr. Borress gives you a good report. Promise?"

"I promise."

"You're my girl."

"I better be."

"Keep the bed warm for me."

"Always."

Jana kissed the phone then changed into a peach sweater, jeans, and strappy sandals. *Put this out of your mind until tomorrow.* She peeked in on B.J. across the hall then hurried down the spiral staircase. She went out the French doors in the kitchen passing the hot tub, swimming pool, and cabana. Then she walked through the gardens, past the stables, over the tiny bridge covering the stream, and through the woods to the thatched-roof cottage with its bright blue shutters. Before she could rap at the wooden door, Bove opened it and stood in the doorway like a prize on a television game show. His black hair was combed back, causing his emerald eyes to sparkle in the setting sun. The skin-tight cream-colored polo shirt and chinos barely contained his rippling muscles. Jana tried not to notice.

"Haven't you gotten accustomed to the way I look by now?" Bove asked with a grin on his handsome face.

Jana thought fast. "I was admiring the sun so low in the sky."

Bove's dimples appeared. "That's what you were admiring, huh?"

"Are you going to make me stand outside my own cottage?"

"Can I trust you behind this closed door?"

"I'm wearing a chastity belt." Jana entered the cozy cottage and sat on the brown suede sofa next to the brick fireplace. "I can see why all those women left you, Bove."

"But Jana Lane stayed by my side. You really are every boy's best friend." He handed her a glass of white wine, picked up his own, and joined her on the sofa.

Jana took in the indescribable scent. She glanced over at the kitchenette counter set for two. "Something smells fantastic."

"Lobster with brie and oyster mushrooms appetizer, ginger butternut squash soup, and beet and feta cheese salad. The main course is filet of flounder stuffed with Portobello mushrooms, brown rice, red lentils, and baby kale in a sesame balsamic reduction. Red velvet chocolate raspberry lava cake is for dessert."

Jana laughed. "I take it back. The women who left you were insane."

They toasted and Bove said, "To solving the case."

"Or getting so overweight we never work again." She took a sip of wine then rested her glass on the leather trunk. "How did you cook all that in this small kitchenette?"

"From years of experience living alone."

Jana smirked. "Have you brought Cindi here yet?"

He took a sip. "Cindi?"

"Don't play coy with me, Bove. Cindi salivates into her makeup kit whenever you walk on set."

He crossed his foot over one knee. "I hadn't noticed."

"Bull! You eat it up like a dog at a cancelled wedding banquet."

"I didn't realize it bothered you."

"It doesn't bother me." *Why did my voice jump up two octaves?*

He tweaked her nose. "Could have fooled me."

Time to change the subject. "Aren't we supposed to be discussing the murders?"

Resting his glass next to Jana's, Bove said, "All right. Cindi didn't do it."

"How do *you* know? You weren't even there."

"She doesn't seem like the type of person who would hurt anyone."

"Because she's hot for you?"

"There's that." He smiled. "And she doesn't have a motive for wanting to kill Christa, her agent, or her uncle."

"But *somebody* does.

Bove sat back on the sofa. "I was outside with B.J. Who was near the staircase before Nick fell?"

Jana played it back in her mind. "Your girlfriend."

"Karen?"

"Cindi. But Karen was there, too—with Herm of course, who was pretty hot under his flannel shirt that Nick couldn't remember his lines."

"Does that happen when an actor gets older?"

Thanks, Bove. "Not so far, miraculously."

"I learned my lines like plays in football."

"Whatever works."

Bove sighed. "Clearly Karen and I don't work."

"Have you two filed divorce papers yet?"

"Karen has. I signed willingly."

"Sorry, Bove."

"No you're not."

"Okay, I'm not. Karen seems like a self-serving opportunist. When your gravy train ran out, she hitched her hopeful star to Herm's wagon."

"But it didn't get her anywhere—except in Herm's bed. Christa still has the lead nurse role on the episode, and Karen is still DOA Nurse One."

"And though Herm was frustrated with Nick, if every director killed an actor on his set who flubbed his lines, there would be no actors left."

"Is there anyone else who had a grudge against Nick?"

"Nick and Hyo had an argument earlier today."

"About what?"

"Nick *said* it was about their divergent acting techniques, but he was lying."

"Sounds like a little Jana Lane interrogation is in order with Hyo."

Jana slid to the edge of the sofa. "But there doesn't have to be a motive for killing Nick."

"Because the killer pushed Christa first?"

"That and like Stu, Nick was loved by Christa. What if the killer is going after people Christa loves in an effort to punish her?"

"For what?"

Jana tented her fingers. "She seems to have come around since, but Christa said something hurtful to Hyo, Aisha, Alaster, and Siobhan. She did the same with Missy. Christa and Andrew also insulted Simon."

Bove rested his arm on the back of the sofa and Jana smelled pine. "As they say, you can take the backwaters out of the girl but not the girl out of the backwaters. And Christa's husband is certainly no charmer."

"But he seems devoted to Christa, and she appears to adore him. I can't imagine Andrew would hurt Christa. He saved her from falling today!"

"It seemed to me that Andrew saw Nick as competition for Christa's affections, and for managing Christa's career."

"I agree. And I think Andrew felt the same way about Stu Silverman." Jana groaned. "But he wouldn't push then save Christa." She rubbed her temples. "There's something we're missing, Bove."

"How about that prop kid, Jason Franks?"

"Christa said he looked familiar to her. But he didn't seem to know her or have anything against her."

"He seems to spend a lot of time listening in on other people's conversations."

"So do I. Besides, I've seen him spend most of his time with Missy, which seems more than fine with Missy."

"An on set romance, huh?"

Jana couldn't resist. "Like you and Cindi."

"One more Cindi remark and no dinner for you."

"My lips are sealed—until dinner."

They ate the delicious dinner by candlelight. Jana helped Bove clean up then said goodbye to him at the cottage door. "Thank you for an amazing meal."

"My pleasure." He leaned into the doorway, and his bicep expanded like a melon. "Isn't this where the man kisses the woman goodnight?"

"Don't you want to save it for Cindi?"

"There's enough of me to go around."

"Goodnight, Bove."

He held her hand. "Are you sure you don't want to stay over. I get lonely all by myself in this cottage."

"You'll survive. Enjoy your day off."

He called out after her, "What are you doing tomorrow?"

Tears welled up in Jana's eyes. She tried every acting technique she knew, but she couldn't stop them from falling onto her cheeks.

Bove's handsome face registered concern. "What's wrong?"

"I'm fine." She wiped her face with the back of her arms. "Probably just allergies."

"What is it? Tell me."

He can see through me like cellophane. "I can't, Bove. Not right now."

"Please come back inside and sit with me."

"This isn't the time, Bove. I'll tell you about this soon."

"What can I do?"

"Be my friend."

Bove wrapped his arms around her. "I'm always here for you, Jana. You mean more to me than..." He stopped himself.

She enjoyed the warmth of his touch, as if funneling in his strength. Finally, she pulled away, kissed him on the cheek, and said goodnight.

Jana walked along the lake and through the woods. The sunset exploded fireworks of crimson, marigold, and violet in front of her. By the time she reached the stables, the sky had turned gray. She heard footsteps.

Jana quickened her step. The footsteps grew louder. Turning around, all she saw was gray. *Stay calm, girl. It's probably just a friendly squirrel or a pesky raccoon.* Jana passed over the tiny bridge and picked up the pace. The footsteps grew closer. Using the quick climbing technique she learned for *Going Ape*, Jana kicked off her sandals and dug her feet into the deepest crevices of a nearby tree. When she reached a good distance for look-out, she scanned her property. Seeing nobody, she climbed down the tree, grasped her sandals, and continued walking. Again she heard footsteps. "Is somebody following me?" When she received no reply, Jana used the quick sprint she learned for *Indian Princess*, raced to the rear of her mansion, shut the French door behind her, and scurried up the spiral staircase.

Once she was in bed, she cried herself to sleep.

****

Jana Lane ran down the hospital corridor certain that someone was following her. When the sound of footsteps grew louder, she snapped her head back but saw no one. She continued down the hallway with the clamor of heavy breathing pounding in her ears. Approaching the nurses' station, Jana hid behind the desk. When her breathing returned to normal, she rose and was covered by a shadow.

Gasping for air, Jana rested her back on the gold circular headboard and tried to breathe in for a count of three and out for a count of six. Following a few minutes of deep breathing, she made her way into the bathroom then changed into her sweat clothes. The work-out in her home gym made her feel empowered and ready for the day. Jana showered, got B.J. washed and dressed, then they had breakfast. When he was settled in his room in deep conversation with Clownie, she called Devon and Ed then asked to speak to Jackson. Following some chit-chat about the boys, her film, and Jackson's role as congressman, she told her best friend about her recent health challenge. As usual, he made her laugh with his wild sense of humor; however, she noticed the fear and concern hidden in Jackson's voice. She promised to keep Jackson informed of any news then hung up the phone.

Next, Jana changed into a tan business suit with shoulder pads and gold link jewelry. Upon hearing the doorbell, she headed for the top of the circular staircase just as Missy opened one of the large front doors to Jason Franks.

Dressed in a pretty lemon-colored rayon dress, Missy glowed. "Hi, Jason."

Jason stepped into the cathedral hallway like a teenager on his first date. "Hi, Missy." He rubbed his long nose. "Thanks for letting me stop over." Looking around, he added, "Wow, nice digs. You really live here?"

She nodded. "My room's upstairs, down the hall from B.J.'s."

"Nice." His shoulders slumped. "My parents' house is nothing like this."

"Neither is most people's."

"I guess."

"Are you happy about your day off?"

Jason rubbed his auburn hair. "I'm getting afraid to go to work. First Stu Silverman and then Nicholas Hartford."

"I was pretty close to where it happened."

"Me, too. Did you see him fall?"

Missy nodded. "Christa nearly fell, but Andrew saved her. Nick wasn't so lucky. I wish I saw who pushed them."

"Me, too. I hope the detective and his officers figure out who did it."

Fat chance.

"What are you doing today on your day off?" Missy asked.

"Picking up some more props for the show." He rubbed his palms against his chocolate-colored sweater vest. "How about you?"

"I'm taking care of B.J. as usual." She smiled. "He's so adorable."

Jason smiled. "*You're* adorable."

She blushed. "Not everybody on the set agrees with you."

A line formed across his smooth forehead. "What do you mean?"

She sat on the window seat under the skylight. "Christa and her husband think I'm Satan reincarnated."

"What do they know?"

"Not much if you ask me. I don't like them."

"Then I don't like them either." He sat next to her and put his arm around her shoulders. "Is this okay?"

She nodded. "I like it."

"I like it, too." Jason rested her head on his shoulder. "What do those two have against you?"

Missy's head snapped up. "They know something about me. Something bad."

He laughed. "What could be bad about you? I've never met a girl sweeter than you."

"You wouldn't think I was sweet if you knew the

truth about me."

Jason took her hands. "What truth?"

She looked away. "I haven't told many people."

"How does Christa know?"

Missy groaned. "She overheard me talking to my doctor on the pay phone."

"Are you sick?"

"Yeah."

Beads of sweat lined his forehead. "What's wrong?"

She stood and walked away.

He followed her and wrapped his arms around her. "You can trust me, Missy. After the show is wrapped, I hope we can be…friends."

"I can't tell you."

"Let me take you out to dinner tonight—at the diner. You can tell me about it then."

She shook her head. "I can't tell you this in public."

"Then tell me now!"

So Jason Franks has a temper.

Missy stepped back in reaction to Jason's anger.

He softened. "I'm sorry, Missy. Even though we've only known each other a short time, I…care about you. And if you're interested back, I'd like us to date. Would you like that, Missy?"

"I'd like that a lot."

"Good. Then tell me what's wrong, so I can help you."

"There's nothing you can do to help me."

He took her hand. "Please trust me, Missy?"

She sighed. "You're right. Before this goes any further, I should fess up."

"Fess up to what?"

Tears filled her eyes. "I have a bad disease."

"What is it?"

She took in a deep breath. "It's AIDS."

"AIDS!" He dropped her hand as if it were on fire. "Are you a homosexual?"

"I caught it from my last boyfriend. He was a drug addict"—she grimaced—"before he found the Lord."

The color drained from Jason's face. "Are you sure?"

She nodded. "That's why I got upset when you mentioned having kids."

"And Christa knows?"

Rage filled her eyes. "She sure does."

He took a step backward, nearly knocking into the grandfather clock. Then he looked at his watch. "I...I...think...I better go. I have a large bunch of things to buy—for the show."

Tears ran down Missy's cheeks. "I understand." She opened the door.

"I hope you feel better."

Missy replied to Jason's back, "I'm feeling okay."

Not anymore.

Jason turned to face her. "I'm sorry, Missy."

"Me, too." Missy closed the door and leaned against it.

Jana hurried down the spiral staircase. "It was a shock for him."

Missy looked at Jana with tear-stained eyes. "Christa and Andrew were right. I'm unclean."

"That's not true."

"Yes, it is. Once Christa tells everyone the truth about me, they'll all react just like Jason." The tears fell down her cheeks. "I've lost him forever."

Jana held Missy in her arms. "Jason will come around. And if he doesn't, he's not worth worrying about. You are a part of this household. You mean a great deal to me and to B.J. We need you. We care about you. And this is your home. And you have everyone in my foundation behind you."

"Is that really happening?"

"It sure is. I'm meeting with the lawyers, Simon, and Cornelius today."

Missy smiled weakly. "Do you think the foundation will really make a difference?"

"I sure do. So you, young lady, need to blow your nose, wipe your eyes, and get upstairs to take care of B.J. while I start things in motion. Can you do that?"

Missy nodded.

"Good."

"If you need anything, ask Theresa."

"I will."

Jana took her purse from the end table then opened the front door.

Missy's shaky voice stopped her. "Jana. Christa can talk all she wants about being a Christian. But you're the real deal."

Jana kissed her forehead and hurried out the door.

There was little traffic so early in the morning. Jana drove her sports car downtown and parked in the medical center's lot. Once she had checked in with the receptionist, the nurse brought her into the examining room and asked her to change into a hospital gown. *How ironic. I wore one only yesterday on set. But this is real life.*

Jana sat on the examining table pondering her

future. *Is this a false alarm? Or is this the first lump of many? Will I die of cancer as my mother did when I was thirteen years old? She didn't feel ill at first either. But all that changed with the shooting pains, weight loss, nausea, vomiting, and weakness. Will Brian and I grow old together? Will I see my children graduate from college, marry, have children of their own?*

Dr. Roberta Borress, a tall, thin, dark-haired woman with a long face, entered the room with the tails of her open white coat flapping behind her. "Hello, Jana."

"Hi, Dr. Borress."

"You're not due for a physical for another six months." Dr. Borress examined the chart. "Tell me about this lump."

Trying to maintain her composure, Jana said, "I found it two days ago."

"Is it tender to the touch?"

"No."

"Let's see what we have."

After Dr. Borress examined her, the doctor sat on a stool across from the examining table. "I know you want answers, but I won't have any for you until the results come back from the tests. We'll start with blood work, a mammography, and a needle biopsy. Given your family history, I've asked for a rush on the tests. I should have all the results back in two days."

Jana sighed. "How do I get through the next two days?"

"By doing what you normally do and not thinking about this. Can you do that, Jana?"

"I'm an actress after all."

Dr. Borress smiled. "That should come in handy."

Jana made her way throughout the medical building, completing the various tests prescribed by Dr. Borress. When she was through, Jana got dressed and called Brian collect from a pay phone in the corridor. She absorbed his love and support like a sponge, and promised him she would take one step at a time—and call him the second she got the results.

Next, she drove farther downtown to a wood-paneled office, where she and Simon sat behind a long wooden desk. The lawyer sitting opposite them on a leather swivel chair droned on about the various legal components of The Jana Lane AIDS Foundation, which went over Jana's head like the papers in front of her. When the lawyer had finished his lecture and Simon nodded his approval, Jana signed her name more times than in her heyday in Hollywood. The moment Jana could escape, she grabbed Simon's arm and led him outside.

Minutes later, Jana sat on red upholstery in a diner booth opposite Simon and Cornelius. The busboy lay glasses of water on the silver tabletop then stared at Jana, popping his gum.

Simon adjusted the lime scarf over his tangelo jumpsuit. "Something wrong, kid?"

The boy scratched at a freckle on his ear. "Can I have your autograph?"

"Sure."

As Jana signed, Simon said to Cornelius, "This happens everywhere we go."

The boy looked at the cocktail napkin Jana had signed. "Who's Jana Lane?"

Simon snarled like a lion. "The top movie star in America!"

The boy ran a hand through his crewcut and said to Jana, "I thought you were Deborah Harry." Then he walked away.

Simon rose and shouted, "And that's why you're a busboy and not a waiter—or a film critic!"

Cornelius sat him back down.

"I want to talk to the owner of this establishment. They should be honored to have such a big star in their presence!"

"Calm down, Simon." Jana opened her menu. "I can't compete with a rock star."

"Don't give him any ideas." Cornelius put his arm around Simon. "You may be recording a rock tune next, Jana."

"Once *The Detective's Wife* hits the airways, every busboy in America will want your autograph, baby girl." Simon polished the gold glasses hanging around his neck from a silver chain, put them on, then perused the menu. "I just hope shooting resumes tomorrow—and nobody gets *shot*."

A middle-aged woman in uniform arrived. "Hi, I'm—"

"Waitress, who is this?" Simon pointed to Jana, and Jana raised her eyes to the fluorescent lighting.

The woman smiled. "That's Jana Lane."

"Thank you." Simon preened like a peacock.

"I'm Helen Cameron. Vivie and Giles' mom. We met at a PTA meeting last year."

Jana laughed. "Of course. It's nice to see you again, Helen."

"Have you seen this woman's movies?" Simon asked as if the waitress was on the witness stand.

Helen replied, "I don't get out to the movies

much."

Simon was like a dog with a new bone. "But you must have seen Jana Lane's early films."

"I heard of them of course. But my parents wouldn't let me see them."

"Why not?" Simon hollered.

"They were afraid my brother and I would try to imitate some of the stunts Jana and Timmy did in those old movies."

"Shame on your parents." Simon pushed Cornelius' arm away. "That was child abuse."

Helen smiled. "But I bought the whole set on video for my kids who love them."

Simon kissed the woman on the cheek. "You will be getting a good tip, Helen." He pointed at Jana. "Give the check to her."

Once they ordered and Helen served their lunches, Simon dug into his triple decker sandwich. "Have you figured out who killed Stu and Nick yet, baby doll?"

Jana replied, "Actually, I have a few questions for *you*, Simon?"

"Me?" Simon adjusted his girdle. "What could I know about any of this?"

Jana moved her fork through her cottage cheese and fruit plate. "You were watching the shooting yesterday. Did you see who pushed Christa and Nick?"

Simon covered Cornelius' ears. "I glanced away for a moment when a hunky cameraman crossed my path. When I looked back at the stairwell, Nick was at the bottom of it."

"I heard every word you said." Cornelius waved his turkey sandwich at Simon.

"And you still love me." Simon kissed Cornelius'

cheek, and Cornelius blushed.

Jana said, "When you negotiated my contract for the TV series, did you meet with the woman who greeted us the first day as producer?"

"Yes. Why, baby doll?"

Cornelius wiped mayonnaise off Simon's sunken cheek.

Jana replied, "As we know, a television series has many producers."

Simon nodded. "You're one of them on this show."

"But who owns Nevgere Productions?" Jana asked.

A crease formed between Simon's tweezed eyebrows. "I don't know."

Curiouser and curiouser. "How are preparations going for Friday night at Bowdoin Park?"

Simon replied, "The decorator will appoint each pavilion with red ribbons and red roses."

Cornelius leaned forward. "I've lined up the musicians who will play at the second pavilion. Dancing will be at the third pavilion."

"And the caterers are all set for the fourth pavilion," Simon added. "Seating is at the fifth pavilion with a microphone for your speech, baby girl. I invited everyone from the show"—Simon lifted his small chin—"and from my contact list of anyone who is anyone, meaning rich and generous."

Cornelius explained, "The first pavilion will be set up with a table full of brochures and the itinerary for the Jana Lane AIDS Foundation."

"It all sounds wonderful." She kissed their cheeks. "You two are miracle workers."

"No argument here," Simon replied.

"How are tour preparations coming along?" Jana

asked.

Simon answered, "We've booked the first month beginning in two weeks. Hyo, Alaster, Aisha, and Siobhan will go into rehearsal next week. They're quite talented. *And* they are relieved they won't have to hide their status as two couples—two gay couples—as Christa Bianca wants them to on the television set."

"Christa's coming around," Jana replied.

"Hah! So is Gorbachev," Simon said.

They finished their lunch then Simon and Cornelius took off on Cornelius' motorcycle to head home and book more tour dates. Jana drove to the local library. She parked then made her way to the historic stone edifice, up the stairs, through the wooden door, past the fireplace, and to the information desk. "Hi, Melanie."

"Hi, Jana." The young woman looked up over her large round glasses. "It took me a few phone calls, and the use of the Freedom of Information Act, but I believe I have the information you phoned about."

Jana reached for the photocopy. "May I keep this?"

"It's all yours."

"Thanks, Melanie."

"Any time." Melanie winked. "Just let me know when we should change the name of the public library to 'Private Eyes.'"

Jana shared a laugh with Melanie. As she quickly read, her legs wobbled. She sat on the window seat overlooking the green lawn. *The owner of Nevgere Productions is Andrew Bianca.*

Chapter 7

"Are you doing okay?" Bove asked with a sweet expression on his handsome face.

"I am now." Jana squeezed his hand.

"Listen up, everyone." Herm Fenton stood in front of the large meeting room and called his cast and crew to attention.

Jana sat on a sofa with B.J. on her lap. Bove sat to their right and Missy to their left. Having awoken from her usual nightmare, Jana skipped her morning workout due to sensitivity from the needle biopsy. She arrived with her entourage at the makeshift studio, where she headed for her dressing room to change into her familiar-looking hospital garb. *It's hard not to think about my health when working in a hospital.*

In his flannel shirt and jeans, Herm pointed to a young police officer sitting alone in a corner of the room. "The police are here to watch over Christa and make sure no further…incidents occur."

Jana noticed Christa and Andrew sitting on a loveseat nearby. Andrew pushed his glasses up his nose and put his arm around his wife. Christa looked shaken.

Herm picked at a pockmark on his neck. "We'll start today by shooting cross-overs with the supporting cast doing business in the hospital corridors. With Nick…deceased, we need to reshoot the hospital administrator's scene with Jana. We only saw his shadow in the other scenes, so we don't need to reshoot those."

Alaster, in his hospital whites, asked, "Who will play the role of the hospital administrator?"

Sitting next to Alaster, Hyo said, "Alaster was cast as the doctor, so he should move up to Nick's role."

Aisha and Siobhan, sitting across from them, nodded their agreement.

Herm bit at the flesh where his fingernails once resided. "Karen Evans has been cast in the role."

Bove groaned.

In a navy blue business suit quite different from her usual revealing leather garb, Karen sat on an easy chair next to Herm and beamed like a floodlight.

Aisha asked, "Was that approved by the producers?"

Herm glared at her. "The executive producer agreed."

Andrew Bianca.

Herm continued. "Having a woman hospital administrator will help bring in the female viewer demographic. We will also reshoot the Nurse One scene we previously shot with Karen."

"Who will play *that* role?" Siobhan asked.

Herm replied, "Cindi Vizard."

All heads turned to the makeup woman dressed in a nurse's uniform with her blonde hair pulled back in a bun and a petrified look on her pretty face.

"But she's not a member of Screen Actors Guild!" Aisha said.

"Yes she is." Herm looked down at his notes. "A production assistant will come for Cindi and Jana when the hospital room set is lit." Herm and Karen whispered together.

As Missy took charge of B.J., Bove turned to Jana with his muscles bulging out of his polo shirt and chinos. "In talking with Cindi, I found out she did some acting in New York City."

"What kind of acting?" Jana asked.

"Commercials. So I recommended her to Herm," Bove explained.

Really?

Simon, standing behind Jana in a raspberry jumpsuit and lime scarf, whispered in her ear, "Looks like you have competition, baby doll." Then he escaped for seconds at the breakfast table.

Cindi walked over to Bove. He rose as she took his hand in hers. "Thank you for the random act of kindness."

"It wasn't random." Bove's dark eyes twinkled. "I think you'll be perfect in the role."

Cindi turned to Jana. "I'm a wreck about getting back into acting."

"You didn't mention you were an actor"—Jana stood and looked at Bove—"to me."

Cindi looked down at her white shoes. "I got a gig doing makeup for a producer of television commercials in New York City. When an actress didn't show, I held up a bottle of shampoo and smiled at the camera."

I can see how your vast résumé would impress Bove.

"I'll bet you sold lots of shampoo."

Down, boy. Jana asked Cindi, "Would you like to run our lines for the scene?"

Cindi held her stomach and called out over her shoulder, "Right after I come out of the ladies' room."

Jana turned to Bove. "I thought you were an actor now, not a casting director."

Bove winced. "Don't actors make casting suggestions when an immediate replacement is needed?"

Jana replied, "Sure, but won't it be uncomfortable for you to have your ex-wife as the hospital administrator and your potential new wife as Nurse One?"

Bove placed his mouth near her ear and Jana smelled pine. "Don't worry. You'll always be the best woman for me."

Jana thought about Brian. "I'm being silly." *And jealous.* "You did a nice thing for Cindi, Bove. I'm proud of you." She softened her voice. "While you and Cindi were planning her career, I found out something interesting about our employer." Jana was distracted by loud voices nearby.

Hyo said to Alaster sitting next to him, "You were cast legitimately as a doctor. *You* should have been moved up to the hospital administrator."

Aisha turned to Siobhan at her side, "And you were cast as a nurse. Nurse One is a small role, but it's flashier than *yours*."

"Excuse me." Jana left Bove and walked over to the two couples. "Simon tells me you are all starting rehearsal next week for the fundraising tour."

Aisha replied, "We're really excited."

"Thank you for the opportunity," her girlfriend added.

"My pleasure," Jana replied with a warm smile.

Hyo grumbled, "I'm sure we'll feel more appreciated there than we do here."

Alaster put a hand on his boyfriend's knee, looked around the room, then quickly took it off. He explained to Jana, "Hyo and Aisha are…surprised about the new casting developments."

Aren't we all. "Tomorrow is our last day of shooting. So let's all pitch in and finish the episode. Can we do that?"

The four of them nodded like children being asked to finish their peas and carrots.

"Good." Jana locked eyes with Hyo. "May I speak with you a moment?"

"Of course."

Jana led Hyo to a quiet corner of the room. "Hyo, what were you and Nick really arguing about yesterday?"

Hyo averted her gaze. "Our acting techniques, like Nick said."

Use the fabrication technique from School Spy to get to the truth. "Were you and Nick having a lovers' spat?"

Hyo's face turned scarlet. "Of course not! Just because we're both gay, that doesn't mean—"

"So Nick was gay." *And he never told his niece.* "Is that what you two were arguing about?"

Hyo sighed. "The older generation should have come out to pave the way for us. They stayed hidden and closeted. Now we have to as well."

Jana put her arm around him. "Hyo, each generation reveres and reviles the one before it. And every generation makes its mark. Perhaps your generation's mark will be honesty and pride." She smiled. "Let's start with the AIDS show tour. Deal?"

He returned the smile. "Deal."

Jana spotted Christa in her nurse costume and Andrew in a suit too large for him. "See you on set, Hyo." Jana walked over and stood in front of the sofa.

Christa patted the seat next to her and Jana sat. "Will you come to Uncle Nick's wake tonight, Jana?"

"Of course."

Remember how you identified the ape that pushed you in Going Ape? "Christa, how did the hands feel that pushed you on the staircase? Were they small, large, thin, thick? Did you feel short nails or long nails?"

Christa closed her eyes. "They were strong and they felt...angry." She opened her eyes. "Does that make sense?"

Jana remembered back to her own past attacks. "I'm afraid it does."

Christa's eyes widened. "And the person wore a ring. I remember feeling it against my back."

Most people wear a ring, including me. She looked over at the police officer. "Rivera was smart to post a police officer here."

Andrew pushed his glasses up his nose. "Christa doesn't need anyone watching over her, but me."

Hasn't worked too well so far. "Andrew, I found out you own Nevgere Productions. Why is it that you didn't mention that to anyone?"

"I can explain that, Jana." Christa held Andrew's hand. "When *On My Own* became the little indie movie that could move from art houses to the big screen, Stu recommended I invest the money I made."

Andrew interrupted her. "So I came up with the idea of starting our own production company, like the big Hollywood high-rollers do."

"But Stu thought we should start small by

producing a television show," Christa said. "To build what Stu called my 'household familiarity.' And I wanted to give my Uncle Nick a role in hard times. Stu, Andrew, and I really liked the script when we read it, and we were so thrilled when you signed on to star in the series."

Andrew added, "And it only committed Christa to one week. After the series is a hit, we can use the money to produce movies starring Christa Bianca." Andrew kissed her forehead. "Christa came up with the name of the company."

Jana asked, "Why is only Andrew's name listed as owner and not yours, Christa?"

"It's in the Bible," Andrew answered. "A woman can't take a leadership position."

But she can star in movies?

"We're just following the Lord's will," Andrew explained. "He's brought us this far."

Hyo, Alaster, Aisha, and Siobhan stood before them. "Excuse me, Mr. Bianca," Hyo said. "Did you just say you own the production company that is producing this series?"

"That's right," Andrew rose.

"That explains a lot," Alaster mumbled to Hyo.

"Excuse me?" Andrew asked.

Siobhan tried to hold back Aisha who blurted out, "That explains why none of us were given the opportunity to read for the role of the hospital administrator."

Andrew laughed. "I wanted to fire the lot of you. But Christa talked me out of it." Andrew leaned in to them. "We've had two cast replacements since then. I'll be happy to have four more."

Jana stood. "My contract gives me creative control, including in casting. Nobody will be fired."

A production assistant and her squawking walkie-talkie led the two gay couples to the set.

Jana felt a strong hand on her arm lead her a few feet away.

"Did I hear that Andrew Bianca owns Nevgere Productions?" Bove asked.

Jana nodded.

Simon was at her other side. "I'm going to ask Mr. Producer about his next project." Simon cornered Andrew at the food table.

Jana squeezed Bove's forearm. "We'll catch up later." She walked over and sat facing Christa. "Why didn't you tell me you and Andrew are my employers?"

Christa replied, "I didn't want Uncle Nick to know we hired him. And if I had told you, there might have been distance between us—like boss and worker." She took Jana's hand. "I consider us friends, and I hope we can remain friends after we wrap."

Jana sighed. "I doubt Andrew would like that."

"You don't know him like I do."

Jana slid to the edge of her seat. "But since the money you invested in Nevgere Productions is *your* money from your last film, why is Andrew listed as the sole owner?"

"Ever since he found me crying in that cloakroom, Andrew has been taking care of me—including dealing with business things I don't want to understand."

"Christa, show business is a business. It's the wise participant who enters it with as much knowledge and control as possible."

"I want to be on camera!" B.J. plopped himself

down on his mother's lap.

You're definitely a Lane.

Christa giggled. "And the camera loves you, B.J. Because you are a sweetheart." She tweaked his nose.

Missy arrived out of breath. "I'm sorry, Jana. B.J. got away from me."

"No problem." Jana hugged her son to her chest.

"Missy, can I talk to you?" Jason Franks ran a hand through his hair.

Missy gave the lint on her Kelley-green skirt—and Jason—the brush off. "You don't have to talk to me, Jason."

"I'd like to." Jason's eyes pleaded.

Jana said, "I can watch, B.J."

B.J. chimed in with, "Christa can watch B.J., too!"

"You got it." Christa winked at B.J. When Andrew returned, Christa took her husband's hand. "I can't wait until God blesses us with one of our own."

Andrew nodded. "Andrew Jr."

Missy turned a shoulder to Jason. "You made yourself clear last night, Jason."

He scratched at the collar of his black turtleneck. "Please hear me out, Missy."

Missy sighed and followed Jason a few feet away.

"I know I've seen that guy somewhere before." Christa shrugged. "Maybe he just has that kind of a face."

As B.J. and Christa played peek-a-boo on the sofa and Andrew went off to talk to Herm, Jana couldn't help overhearing Missy and Jason.

Jason said, "What you told me last night—"

"Made you disgusted and repulsed. I understand."

Jason grabbed Missy's wrist. "You're right. It did."

Missy pulled her arm away. "You don't want to touch me, Jason. I'm diseased."

"I know. I mean, that's what I thought, until I went home and called my family doctor. He explained you can't catch AIDS from touching someone."

"Jason, you don't have to talk to your doctor. You're not the one with AIDS."

"But *you* are. Someone I like, a great deal." He rubbed his long nose. "Missy, I'm sorry about the way I reacted last night."

"It's okay. I understand."

"No, it's not okay. I was unfeeling and insensitive. I thought about myself, other people, and even the disease. I thought about everyone and everything... except you."

She straightened the collar of her white blouse. "I know what you think about me, Jason. I think the same thing about myself. That's why I had to be honest with you. So you can move on and find someone who isn't going to die."

He flailed his thin arms. "But we're all going to die—someday."

"Not without having kids." Missy's eyes filled with tears.

"My doctor told me there are new treatments coming up. Who knows what will happen five, ten years from now?"

"If I'm still alive."

He took her hands in his. "You can't leave me now, Missy. I just found you. You make me...happy. It feels...right when we're together. I haven't felt comfortable in my own skin for...ever since I can remember. But when we're together, it feels like…home." Jason wrapped his arms around her.

"I don't want to put you through this."

"Please let me help you, Missy."

She backed away from him. "And I don't want to be your charity case."

"You'll be my salvation." Jason looked down at his work boots. "I've done some things in my life that I'm not proud of."

"What things?"

He sighed. "When I was in high school. I got in some trouble."

"For what?"

"Trying to be a big man—when I knew I was nothing of the kind."

"What did you do?"

"Dippy things like pushing smaller guys into their lockers, stealing their lunch money, and saying mean things to make girls cry. I'm embarrassed about it."

"So, you think dating me will be your penance for doing those things?"

"No, Missy." He put his head in his hands. "This is coming out all wrong."

"I think it's coming out all *right*. You don't need to take care of me to gain forgiveness for your past sins. You're free to go and find a healthy girl." Missy ran away.

Bove arrived and took B.J.'s hand. "Come on, B.J., the walkie-talkie is calling for us to head down the hallway to the camera."

"Yeah!"

When they were gone, Jana felt a tap on her shoulder. "Can we go over our scene?" Cindi clutched at her stomach.

"Sure." Jana sat Cindi between Christa and herself. "Whenever you're ready, Cindi."

Cindi blurted out as if someone had a gun to her head, "Is your husband gone?" She looked at Jana like a deer facing a hunting party.

Jana and Christa shared a glance.

"Is something wrong?" Cindi looked from side to side like a criminal surrounded by the police.

Jana said, "Let's go through the scene."

"Okay." Cindi's back stiffened, her eyes bulged out of her pretty face, and her voice became monotone and flat. "Is your husband gone?"

Jana rubbed her temples. "Let's forget the script. You know that Bove plays my husband in the show, right?"

"Uh-huh."

"Look around the room. Do you see Bove?"

Cindi did as Jana instructed. "No."

"So ask me if he's gone?"

"Is Bove gone?" Cindi cringed. "I mean, is your gone husband." She groaned. "Is your husband a goner? Agh!"

Christa looked at Jana with concern. Not giving up, Jana twisted around to face Cindi. "Have you ever felt badly about something you've done? And you wanted to tell somebody about it, but you didn't know how?"

Cindi nodded.

"Then use that feeling and say the words in the scene."

Cindi closed her eyes, took in a deep breath, then stared at Jana. "Is your husband gone?"

Jana replied, "Yes."

She spoke in a frightened whisper. "I've done

something I'm ashamed of. I thought maybe I could talk to your husband about it."

Jana rested a hand on Cindi's shoulder, "Would you like to tell *me* about it?"

Tears filled Cindi's eyes. "I don't think I can."

"You can trust me."

Cindi said between quivering breaths, "I tried to blackmail someone, but it blew up in my face." Terror filled her young face. "And now I'm so afraid."

Jana was mesmerized by Cindi's realistic performance. *Or was it a performance?*

Christa threw her arms around Cindi. "That was wonderful! You are some actress!"

Cindi seemed to return to reality. "Thank you both for helping me."

In the nick of time.

The production assistant squawked. Jana asked the returning Missy to take care of B.J. when he came back from the set. Then Jana and Cindi followed the young woman to the space set up as Jana's hospital room. Jana took off her robe and climbed into the now familiar bed. With no one to do their makeup, Cindi did double-duty. When Herm called for, "Quiet, roll, slate, and action!" Cindi stood at the side of Jana's bed with the quivering folder in her hand. In each take, Jana and Cindi played the short scene as beautifully as in the waiting room.

"Cut! Print! Next scene." Herm seemed surprised and very pleased at Cindi's performance. "Let's move on to the hospital administrator scene down the hall."

Cindi grasped Jana's hand like a lifeboat. "Thank you for helping me, Jana."

"*You* did it, Cindi." Jana smiled. "And you did it

very well."

Bove threw his herculean arms around Cindi. "You were amazing! This is only the start for you."

Cindi melted in Bove's arms. "How can I ever thank you?"

Simon came to the other side of the bed and said to Jana sotto voce, "I'm sure he'll find a way—if you don't move fast, doll face."

The production assistant led Jana, with Simon following, down the hallway to the room used for the hospital administrator's office. Jana secured her robe and sat opposite Karen—looking quite officious in her business suit and shoulder pads. Jana noticed Missy, B.J., Hyo, and Alaster watching.

Cindi applied Jana's and Karen's makeup. "I guess I'm back to makeup girl."

Jana patted Cindi's shoulder.

Herm called for rehearsal. Jana and Karen played the scene where Jana fabricates her displeasure as a patient in order to confront the administrator with her suspicions about the businesswoman's illegal activities. Unlike Nick, Karen knew her lines, but she said them flatly without much feeling or conviction. *This scene is about as exciting as watching paint dry—in a nursing home.*

Once they had finished going through the scene, Herm called Karen over to a corner of the room and whispered something in her ear. She nodded then returned to her seat. Herm shouted, "Roll! Slate! Action!" This time Karen was like a tigress, bobbing and weaving to Jana's inquiries, then attacking with claws extended in the face of Jana's suspicions. When Herm called, "Cut!" Jana was out of breath from their verbal sparring.

Herm moved on to the close-up shot on Karen. Jana didn't think Karen's performance could get more vibrant, but Karen lunged into the scene like a prizefighter, leaning over her desk, baiting Jana, confronting her, and nearly attacking her. Jana used every ounce of her skill as an actress to be an equal partner in the ring.

When the scene was finished, Herm called for a break to reset for the next location. Simon was at Herm's side like a rash. "When are you going to shoot Jana's close-up?"

Herm looked down his nose at Jana's agent. "We don't need one."

"We most certainly *do* need one."

"I have what I need."

Simon didn't budge. "I don't. And if I don't, my client doesn't. And without my client, you have a blue sky without a star in sight."

Herm shouted, "Let's set up for the close-up on Jana."

Jana steadied herself for another round with Karen. Again the two of them battled like champions. When the scene was finished, Herm kissed Karen then hurried down the hallway shouting, "Let's set up for the next shot."

Karen shook Jana's hand and nearly cracked the bones. "Nice job. We make a good team."

I'll give you a call if I ever become a professional wrestler.

Karen said to Bove, standing nearby, "How'd I do?"

His eyes turned into slits. "You were quite the

performer, as always."

Karen grinned. "Thanks. I didn't know you still cared."

"I don't."

"So what else is new?" Karen walked off in a huff.

Jana was exhausted and happy for the break. As everyone scattered in all directions, Bove offered his hand. Rising, Jana said, "I wonder what Herm whispered in Karen's ear before we shot?"

As they walked down the hallway, Bove smirked. "My guess is Herm told Karen to play Mistress Karen."

Suddenly they heard a scream.

Following the sound, Jana ran down the hallway with Bove at her heels. She looked into the open supply closet and found Christa lying still on the gray floor.

Chapter 8

Christa Bianca lay in her white nurse's outfit, sprawled out on the supply room floor with a pool of blood on her right side. A supply cabinet lay on her left side with medical supplies strewn on the floor. Jana started to enter, and Bove pulled her back. "Don't contaminate the crime scene." He ran down the hallway calling for help.

Jana said, "Christa? Can you hear me?" She breathed a sigh of relief when Christa slowly sat up on one elbow. "Don't move, Christa. Stay right there. Help will be here soon."

Christa sat up slowly. "I was…walking down the hall…to watch some of your scene with Karen. Someone pushed me…from behind."

"I heard you scream."

"I must have…passed out."

A production assistant arrived, followed by Bove. "Can you walk?"

"I think so." Christa rose shakily, held onto the production assistant's extended hand, and slowly took the few steps out of the supply closet.

Jana noticed the gash on Christa's leg. "Her leg is cut."

"I need the first-aid kit," the production assistant squawked into the walkie-talkie.

The nurse consultant appeared.

"Call an ambulance," Bove said.

"No need." Andrew Bianca ran down the hallway and coiled his arm around his wife's waist. He looked at her leg. "Christa will be fine. We got scrapes like that from falling down the mountain when we were kids."

Jana pointed to the blood on the supply closet floor. "Christa's lost a lot of blood."

Andrew shouted, "Then let's get her into one of these offices and bandaged up before she loses any more."

Holding onto Andrew on one side and the production assistant on the other, Christa walked down the hallway and into an office with the nurse consultant following.

Jana stood at the doorway to the supply closet and looked around the room.

Bove said, "I woke the police officer who was supposed to have been watching her, and asked him to call Rivera."

Jana didn't move.

"What is it?"

"I counted eleven pairs of rubber gloves on the floor."

"Okay."

"Not ten or twelve, which would generally come in a box. And the drawers are open."

"Come again?"

"In *The Sweet Candy Striper*, someone pushed Timmy into the supply closet. The fall caused his leg to bleed, too"—she scanned the blood on the floor—"in just about the same place."

"Okay?"

"But the drawers weren't open."

Joe Cosentino

"What the hell are you talking about?"

Jana explained, "Christa told me someone pushed her from behind. She must have fallen into the supply cabinet, cut her leg, and blacked out. So the alcohol, bed pans, cotton, rubber gloves, tourniquets, and needles fell from the supply cabinet onto the floor."

"Right."

"But why are two drawers open in the *second* cabinet farther away?"

The young police officer arrived. "Please clear this area and go back to the meeting room.

Jana asked the officer, "Who else was in the meeting room when you woke up and noticed Christa was missing?"

"The food service people, Andrew Bianca, and two women in white outfits."

"What did they look like?"

"A dark woman and a redhead."

"Did you call Rivera?" Bove asked.

The police officer nodded. "He'll be here shortly."

Then we'll have two incompetent officers running the investigation.

Jana nearly bumped into the white column in the hallway as she and Bove walked to the small room where Christa was being treated by the nurse consultant. Once Jana was confident Christa would be fine, she walked back to the main meeting room with Bove at her side. Upon finding Missy and B.J., she wrapped her arms around her son.

"More camera for B.J.?"

She kissed his cheeks. "Not right now, B.J."

Herm stood at the front of the room. "Attention, everyone."

The various clusters of conversation halted at intervals.

When it was quiet, Herm said, "As most of you have probably heard, Christa Bianca was injured." Once the gasps died down, he scratched the back of his neck. "But she's all right."

Christa entered the room with a bandaged leg, holding onto Andrew for support. Everyone applauded, which caused her cheeks to turn red. She blew a kiss to the crowd then sat next to Andrew on a loveseat.

Thank goodness.

B.J. said to Jana, "Did Christa fall down and go boom?"

Jana replied, "Yes. But she's fine, B.J."

B.J. ran over to Christa and handed her his rag doll. "Clownie will make you feel better."

"Thank you, B.J.!" Christa hugged Clownie to her chest.

Clearly a man of few words, Herm said, "Let's all break for lunch."

The police officer added, "Don't anybody leave. Detective Rivera would like to speak to each of you. And please don't go near the hospital supply cabinet on your set. I've taped it off. Thank you."

Bove went over to speak with the police officer.

Once a detective…

Simon appeared and squeezed Jana's arm. "Are you all right, baby doll?"

"I'm fine, Simon."

"Thank the TV gods." He hurried off to be the first in line at the food table.

Jason approached Jana and Missy with a worried look on his young face. "When I heard someone was hurt and bleeding, I thought it might be you, Missy."

Missy took a step away from him. "Don't worry, Jason. I didn't bleed on anybody and get them sick."

"That's not what I meant."

Jana held his arm. "Can I speak with you a moment?"

"Sure."

"Missy, please watch B.J."

"Of course." Missy glared at Christa. "As soon as he's finished talking to Christa."

Jana walked with Jason to the window seat. "Please, join me." Once they were seated, Jana asked, "Was part of your job as prop master to fill the storage closet in the hallway?"

He nodded. "Herm shot a scene in there this morning."

"Do you know who was in that scene?"

"The Asian guy playing the orderly and the red-headed lady who's a nurse."

"Hyo and Siobhan. What props did you need for the scene?"

He whistled. "Lots of things. I had to fill one cabinet with stacked up bedpans, boxes of cotton, bottles of alcohol, a package of needles, a box of rubber gloves, and tourniquets."

"How many rubber gloves come in a box?"

"Twelve."

"And the other cabinet?"

He took a piece of paper out of his pants' pocket and read, "A box of bandages, a package of razor blades, bottles of aspirin." Jason looked worried. "Did I forget something?"

"No. You did fine."

Jason swallowed hard. "Was that the room where someone was pushed?"

Jana did a double-take. "How did you know someone was pushed?"

"I heard the police officer talking about it."

"It was Christa."

"Oh."

Is he smiling? "When was the last time you were in the supply closet?"

He looked at his watch. "About two hours ago."

"When you left, were any drawers in the far cabinet from the door left open?"

"No. I shut them all."

"Did you leave the door to the supply closet open?"

"Uh-huh."

"Where were you over the last fifteen minutes?"

"In the meeting room. Having a pop."

'Pop' is generally used in rural areas. We say 'soda' in this part of the country. "The police officer said only the food service people, Andrew, Siobhan, and Aisha were in the meeting room at that time."

He shrugged. "I guess I was in the men's room." Holding her arm, he asked, "Since I answered your questions, can you answer mine?"

Jana rested back on the loveseat. "All right."

His blue eyes bore into hers. "I'm worried about Missy."

"She's been feeling fine."

"That's not what I meant." His thin fingers curled around one another. "I said some pretty stupid things to her last night. And now she won't talk to me. Do you think you could plead my case to her?"

Jana smiled. "You don't need me to do that,

Jason."

His voice broke like an aging choir boy's. "I think I love her."

"Then hold onto that."

Rivera arrived and spoke with the police officer, Bove, and Herm. Then he headed toward Jana. "May I speak with you?"

"I better check on the props for the next scene." Jason was gone.

Jana rose and stood opposite Rivera.

"I am inches away from closing down this production, Mrs. Otley. The only reason you are still in operation is Mr. Fenton promised me the shooting will finish by the end of the day tomorrow, and I want to keep the attacker on these premises until we catch him."

Jana smiled. "Then we start shooting the next episode a week later."

"If I give clearance." He pointed to an easy chair. "Please sit down."

Jana obeyed.

Rivera took the easy chair opposite. "Did you see anything out of the ordinary when you found Mrs. Bianca in the supply closet?"

"Not really."

He laughed. "Come on, Mrs. Otley. Surely the *Girl Detective* noted some clue or other to laud over my head."

Jana thought about how she found Christa. "*The Little Shop Girl*!"

"Excuse me?"

"I need to go into the room next door to the supply closet."

"Why?"

"I'll tell you after I examine that room."

Rivera sighed. "Follow me."

Jana walked with Rivera into the hallway past the supply closet to the room next door, where she and Karen had shot their scene. She searched around the room and stopped at a prop bookcase full of cardboard front books. She slid the bookcase a few inches, revealing a door. Jana opened the door as far as she could—into the supply closet. "I knew it! Just like the secret door from my father's office to the vault room in *The Little Shop Girl*."

When she closed the door, Rivera asked, "What is your earth-shattering clue?"

"Due to the bookcase, this door is not visible in this room. The same holds true for the opposite side of the door in the supply closet. There's a screen covering it on the other side."

"So?"

"I assumed Christa's assailant had to come from the meeting room into the hallway to push her from behind. Your police officer told me very few people were sitting in the meeting room just before Christa was pushed."

"Where were they?"

"Many of them had just watched the scene I shot with Karen Evans—in this room. So any of them could have used this door to enter the supply closet to the hallway and push Christa."

He smirked. "Your theory has a hole in it, Mrs. Otley. Mrs. Bianca said she was pushed from *behind*."

"It would take only seconds for someone to exit the supply closet and hide behind the column adjacent to it. I realized that when I nearly bumped into that column earlier. So anyone involved in the scene, or watching it, could have gone through this door into the supply closet, out the supply closet door, and hidden in the hallway behind the column waiting for Christa." She paced. "The attacker probably wore rubber gloves, which explains the pair missing from the floor—"

"What pair?"

"There are twelve in a box, not eleven. But what concerns me are the two open drawers."

Rivera took his notepad from his suit jacket pocket. As he scratched his eyebrows, the notepaper became full of white flakes. "The two open drawers?"

She nodded. "It's just like in *The Pirate Princess*."

He rolled back his eyes. "Please explain to the detective who hasn't seen all of your old movies, Mrs. Otley."

"The pirate forced me to show him the secret drawer in the treasure chest onboard ship, which I did— just before I bit his wrist, took his knife, and kicked him down to the deck below."

Rivera groaned. "Mrs. Otley, what does this have to do with Mrs. Bianca's attack?"

"The assailant had pushed Christa to the floor. She was out cold, bleeding. So the attacker or attackers put on a pair of rubber gloves, knocked over the first supply cabinet, and rummaged through the drawers of the back supply closet looking for a razor to slash Christa's throat, a bandage to strangle her, or an overdose of drugs to poison her."

"What stopped him?"

"Before she fainted, I heard Christa scream. My footsteps must have scared off whoever attacked her."

"Did you see anyone running down the hallway?"

"No, but I wouldn't have to—if the attacker or attackers left by way of the back closet door into this office."

He jotted a note then snapped the notepad shut. "I will question each individual about this in the solarium."

"With the pandemonium of actors and technicians racing around after the scene was shot, I doubt anyone will remember seeing anything suspicious. Besides, lighting, sound, and camera equipment were being hoisted out of the office set at the time. Those objects would have covered the action of anyone moving in and out through this door."

"Officer Lesar will serve as Mrs. Bianca's bodyguard."

I hope we have lots of coffee to keep him awake.

"I will radio in for another officer to watch the meeting room, where you should now return."

Jana offered a weak smile. "As always, it's been a pleasure, detective." When she returned to the meeting room, Bove placed a plate full of food into her hands with a fork and napkin.

"What's this?"

"Lunch. Eat it."

Jana looked down at the roasted cauliflower and zucchini, black bean and asparagus tips stuffed avocado, and fontina cheese smothered chicken croquettes. "I can't eat all this."

Bove sat her next to him on a loveseat. "Yes, you can."

She spotted B.J. safe with Missy—and Jason still pleading his case to her. So Jana filled in Bove on her talk with Rivera. "That doorway between the office and supply closet would have provided access for anyone watching our scene to attack Christa."

Bove nodded. "Meaning Herm, Karen, Hyo, Alaster, and sorry, Missy."

"Don't forget your girlfriend, Cindi."

"Any man would forget every other woman when Jana Lane was in view." He wiped a piece of avocado off her chin.

She pushed his hand away and wiped her mouth with her napkin. "When Cindi and I rehearsed our scene before shooting, in order to help her get in the mindset of confessing to blackmail, I asked Cindi to use emotional recall and remember something terrible she had done."

"How did she do?"

"You saw her scene. Either she's the actress of the century, or your new honey has a skeleton in her closet."

Bove shifted in his seat. "Or the attacker could have come from the other direction."

"Meaning Andrew, Aisha, or Siobhan."

"Where was Jason?"

"He 'says' he was in the men's room."

"Did you go in there to check?"

"Very funny."

"Why weren't Andrew, Aisha, and Siobhan watching the scene?"

"I don't know. But I intend to find out." She handed him her half-eaten lunch. Noticing Aisha, Siobhan, and Andrew sitting on the sofa, she stood behind it out of sight.

Andrew's nasal twang said, "You two girls are making a big mistake."

Aisha groaned. "*You're* making a bigger mistake if you think we would *ever* do anything like that."

Andrew sighed. "God made you as women. He is unhappy that you chose the homosexual lifestyle."

"Tell me, Andrew, when did you *choose* the *heterosexual lifestyle?*" Aisha asked.

"Like Eve in the Garden of Eden, you need to come to the Lord," Andrew continued. "As women, your role is to please a man. I can show you how to do that, and your past sins will be forgiven. The last days are coming. You girls need to repent and follow the Lord."

Siobhan replied, "Andrew, if you were the last man on the planet and it was our last day on earth, I wouldn't let you touch us."

"Then you'll burn in Hell for eternity."

"That would be more pleasant than being near you," Aisha shouted.

That's it. I've heard enough. Jana stood over them. "What is going on here?"

Andrew darted up like a rocket. "I've been telling these girls about the trinity."

Siobhan laughed bitterly. "Andrew was talking about a different kind of threesome, Jana."

"And the thought of it makes me want to lose my lunch—for a year." Aisha put her plate down on an end table.

Andrew waved his thin finger at them. "It's a sin to mock the Lord."

Aisha's face hardened. "You're not the Lord, Andrew. You're a pathetic man trying to cheat on his wife with women who aren't interested in men—especially you."

"The Lord will punish you for lying and blaspheming." Andrew turned to Jana. "I was doing my Christian duty by trying to bring these two sinners to the Lord."

"Or to your bed." Siobhan glared at him. "Is there a difference, Andrew?"

Andrew waved his hand in their faces and his shirt cuff raised above his wrist. "The Bible says you two girls are an abomination."

Siobhan chortled. "Hey, Andrew, that tattoo on your arm is an abomination according to your holy book."

Andrew's face turned beet red. "You all think you're so smart. Laughing at my religion, and mocking the sign of love for my wife on my arm. But we'll see who gets the last laugh." He walked back to Christa on the other side of the room.

"He was clearly out of line." Jana sat next to them on the sofa. "I'm sorry that happened to you."

"We've met creeps like Andrew before." Siobhan flipped her auburn locks behind her neck. "Love the sinner, hate the sin, but love me. What a bunch of crap. How do their wives fall for it?"

"Andrew and Christa deserve each other," Aisha added.

Hyo and Alaster returned with plates from the food table. "Was Andrew coming onto you again?" Hyo asked sitting across from them.

Alaster clenched his fist. "I'll take care of that guy. He's had it coming since day one."

Jana pressed on Alaster's shoulder to sit him down next to Hyo. Then she searched the women's faces. "Siobhan, Aisha, why weren't you with Hyo and

Alaster on set when I shot my scene with Karen?"

The two women shared furtive glances.

"We wanted a few minutes alone together," Aisha explained.

"But things didn't work out that way," Siobhan added. "Andrew joined us and started his 'let me make you a woman for the Lord' revulsion."

Alaster said through a tight jaw, "If that creep comes near Aisha and Siobhan again, he's going to answer to me."

"And me," Hyo chimed in.

Jana leaned into them. "Do you all trust me?"

The four of them nodded.

"Good. Then please leave Andrew to me. I'll make sure he doesn't bother any of you again." *Back to the investigation.* "But first, Siobhan and Hyo, I need you to tell me about your scene in the supply closet today."

"It was just a quick chat about the rumors at the hospital of someone selling organs on the black market," Siobhan replied with a shrug.

Jana asked, "Did you carry any props?"

"I had a water pitcher," Siobhan said.

"I got the bedpan," Hyo added. "Not too high tech."

"Did either of you use the far cabinet in the supply closet?"

They shook their heads no.

"Did you know there is a door behind the white screen in that storage room that leads to the office where Karen and I shot our scene?"

Siobhan explained, "We didn't use that part of the storage closet in our scene."

Alaster asked with salad in his mouth, "Is this

about Christa being pushed into the supply closet?"

Jana nodded.

Hyo said, "If you ask me, Andrew did it."

"Why would Andrew do that?" Jana asked.

"To show the little lady who's boss," Aisha replied to nods of agreement from the other three.

"Thank you for your help. Excuse me." Jana walked over to Christa and Andrew on the sofa. "Andrew, may I speak to you a moment?"

Once Jana and Andrew were stationed in front of a window, Jana said, "I overheard what you said to Aisha and Siobhan."

Andrew ran a thin hand through his stringy hair. "When I was telling them about the Lord?"

Jana saw red. "No, when you were making a pass at them."

"You obviously misunderstood what you heard— when you were snooping."

"Then let me make sure *you* understand what *I* am saying now. If you harass, threaten, or proposition another employee on this shoot again, I will contact the unions and file a formal complaint on their behalf. Then I will discuss legal avenues with my agent and my lawyer." She glared at him. "Am I understood, Andrew?"

Rage filled his pale face. "One day you'll have to answer for your blasphemy against the Lord."

Jana was nose to nose with Andrew. "My blasphemy is against you, Andrew, and you alone. And right now I can't think of anyone who is more deserving of it."

The assistant director called lunch over. Jana asked Missy to look after B.J. Then, still in their patient and nurse whites respectively, Jana and Christa followed a production assistant's squawking walkie-talkie down a flight of stairs to what once was the hospital's cafeteria. Andrew, Officer Lesar, and Simon followed a few feet behind them. Jana held Christa's arm. "Are you able to walk all right? Are you sure you can do the scene?" Jana asked.

Christa shushed her. "It'd take more than a skinned knee to keep me from acting." She smiled. "Besides, I have Andrew, my knight in shining armor, and Jana Lane, my guardian angel." Taking Jana's hand, Christa added, "What were you and Andrew talking about before we were called to the set?"

Time to set the cheese to catch a rat? "Christa, while you were pushed into the supply closet, Andrew was in the main meeting room talking to Aisha and Sibohan."

Christa turned back toward Andrew and blew him a kiss. "He told me about that. Andrew is so full of love for the Lord, he can't help witnessing to people."

Take two. "I overheard what he said, and it didn't sound very spiritual to me."

Christa groaned. "Did the lesbian thing come up again?"

Jana nodded. "But not in the way you think."

"I don't understand."

Jana lowered her voice. "Christa, Andrew came on to those two young women."

Christa laughed like a school girl. "Jana, you must have misunderstood. Andrew and I saw the two of them kissing. Besides, Andrew has eyes only for me."

"I know what I overheard."

"Andrew is so passionate about his love for the

Lord; it's easy for people to misunderstand his concern for them." She beamed. "I know the man who wraps his arms around me, puts my head on his chest before I fall asleep each night, and wakes me with hugs and kisses each morning is totally devoted to me, and only me."

They arrived to find the film crew had brought the room back to life with plastic food behind glass counters, a cash register, and tables and chairs around the room. Herm asked Jana and Christa to sit at a table that was lit and positioned with the boom microphone above them. As the assistant director positioned a few extras at tables around them, Jason lay trays of coffee and pie in front of Jana and Christa, sitting opposite each other. When Jason brought fake food to the other tables, Christa sighed. "I wish I could remember where I've seen that guy."

Cindi touched up their makeup.

"We've got our makeup girl back!" Christa said happily.

Did Cindi just scowl at Christa?

Jana and Christa rehearsed the scene where Jana as patient and Christa as head nurse share their thoughts about who at the hospital might be responsible for selling patients' organs on the black market, and murdering the night nurse who uncovered the truth and tried to blackmail him or her. The scene wasn't much of a challenge for Jana as an actor, since in her own life she had been in the position of sorting through clues regarding the identity of a murderer. Christa's role was more difficult since her character was frightened for her own life. As a lighting technician replaced a gel, Jana resumed her investigation.

"Have you thought anymore about why someone

might be doing this to you?"

Christa shook her head no. "I wish whoever is doing it would have left Stu and Uncle Nick alone, and taken me instead." Tears brimmed her eyes.

Jana squeezed her hand.

As Jana and Christa rehearsed, Christa seemed to use her current emotional state in the scene. It was an easy task for Jana to question, pity, and comfort Christa, since the young woman was so distraught. Herm moved on to shoot the long shot, close-up on Jana, and finally the close-up on Christa. With each take, Christa grew more and more upset. Jana felt like a psychiatrist watching Christa release pent up emotions and trauma. *Hopefully this is a good catharsis for you, Christa. It's sure giving us a good performance.* Jana couldn't help thinking of her own health scare as she shared her concerns about the hospital administrator.

Herm seemed pleased as he shouted, "Cut! Wrap!"

Jana placed her arm around Christa and helped her up. "Believe me, Christa. I'm going to find out who is doing this to you."

"Thank you, Jana."

Andrew appeared and grabbed hold of Christa. "I'll take care of my baby."

Christa nestled her head in Andrew's chest, and they left the cafeteria.

Despite Rivera interviewing cast and crew members one at a time in the solarium, the shooting proceeded quickly and efficiently for the rest of the afternoon. When they were released, Jana, Bove, Missy, and B.J. were driven back to Jana's mansion. Bove headed to the guest cottage, and Jana, Missy, and B.J. had dinner in her dining room—a recipe Theresa picked up during a commercial for one of her soap operas.

Jana and B.J. called Devon and Ed at Jackson's. Then with B.J. proclaiming his desire to join his brothers next summer, Jana got B.J. ready for bed, read him—and Clownie—a story, and tucked him in for the night. With Missy on B.J. duty, Jana tiptoed into her bedroom and phoned Rivera for an update on Christa's case. Then she changed into a sapphire one-piece swimsuit and matching cape, climbed down the spiral stairs, and went out the kitchen's French door. Since the sun hadn't set and it was a warm day, Jana rested her cape on the side of the hot tub and jumped into the water. As the warm bubbles caressed and massaged the lower half of her body, she gazed out at the crystal-blue sky watching protectively over the stoic mountains and meandering lake. When her muscles felt exhausted and invigorated at the same time, she pulled herself out of the water, took a thick burgundy towel from the cabana to dry off, and lay on a chaise. She closed her eyes and enjoyed the sun's rays bathing her body.

"You shouldn't lie out in the sun without lotion on."

Jana smelled pine. She opened her eyes to Bove, looking amazingly sexy in sunglasses and a tight sea green bathing suit.

"Where's the lotion?" he asked.

"In the cabana."

Bove returned quickly with a tube of lotion and sat next to her on the lounge chair. She couldn't stop herself from staring at his wide pectoral muscles, rivaling the mountains in the distance. He said, "Stop gaping at me."

"I'm not *gaping*."

"I thought Jana Lane never lied. Turn around." His strong, wide hands rubbed the creamy banana-scented lotion onto her back, then he handed her the lotion. "Put some on the rest of you."

"There's not much sun."

"But it's low in the sky. The best time to get burned. You're shooting tomorrow, remember?"

"What would I do without you?"

"Get sunburned." He sat on the adjoining chase. "Does living in the guest cottage give me pool rights?"

"It appears so." When she was through applying the lotion, she handed the tube back to him.

He rubbed some on his face, arms, abdominals, and legs then gave it back to her. "Can you trust yourself to put some on my back?"

"Won't Cindi get jealous?"

"Cindi can put on her own lotion."

Jana took the tube and slid to the edge of her lounge.

"Go easy, *Jungle Girl*. I worked out at the local gym this morning before we went to the set. I overdid it a bit."

She released some lotion onto her hands then gently kneaded and massaged the rippling muscles on Bove's broad back.

"You're good at this. Were you The Little Masseuse in an old movie?"

"Very funny. I have a husband and three sons remember, the youngest an up-and-coming star?"

"B.J.'s having the time of his life on the set."

"He sure is." Jana's smile turned into a sigh. "I wish I could say the same about Christa." She capped the lotion and put it under her chair.

Bove lay back on his chaise. "You really like Christa, don't you?"

Jana nodded. "I also admire her courage and fortitude. She raised her younger brother and two sisters, and rose from poverty to success."

"But?"

"But what does she see in Andrew? I know he switched course when they were kids and took on the role of her defender, and he's her manager now, but he has Christa totally under his spell." Jana sighed. "She's completely blind to his shenanigans."

"Which are?"

Jana slid to the edge of the chaise. "I overheard Andrew coming on to Aisha and Siobhan."

Bove laughed. "That seems like an exercise in futility."

"You know about them?"

"Of course. And Hyo and Alaster, too. Isn't it obvious?"

Apparently to everyone but me! "Sexual harassment isn't generally about sex or sexuality. In most cases it's about power, and Andrew seems to relish having power over women."

"And as the owner of Nevgere Productions, he's our boss."

"And he used Christa's money to do it."

The old detective was back. "But why would Andrew want to hurt Christa, the love of his life, future mother of Andrew Jr., and his cash cow?"

"But if Andrew is so concerned about Christa, why did he leave her alone to make a play for two other women?"

Bove asked, "Have you spoken to Rivera about the

outcome of his interviews?"

"Rivera told me when he questioned the cast and crew, nobody admitted to seeing anything unusual."

"Did the *Sweet Candy Striper* figure out the clue about the open drawers of the second supply cabinet?"

Jana shook her head. "After the assailant knocked Christa unconscious and turned over the first supply cabinet, he or she must have searched through the two drawers of the second supply cabinet. I asked Rivera earlier on the phone if any of the items in those two drawers looked as if they had been moved or taken, and if anything had visible fingerprints on it."

"And?"

"Lots of things had been moved with no prints on anything. A pair of rubber gloves was missing from the floor."

"Maybe the attacker wore the gloves."

"Then where are they? Rivera told me a razor blade was missing from its pack in the far cabinet's drawer. Where is it? And was the attacker's plan to slash Christa's throat or disfigure her beautiful face? And why didn't he or she push the second cabinet on top of Christa?"

"Maybe there were two attackers, and they argued about what to do next."

"Okay." Jana tented her fingers. "Who might be working together?"

Bove sat facing her. "Herm and Karen."

"But why? With Nick gone, your dominatrix ex-wife has a large, juicy role in the episode. She doesn't need to covet Christa's role any longer. And Herm must want to finish the episode on time and on budget. I know he was frustrated with Nick, but Christa is terrific in her role."

"How about the two couples?"

"They certainly don't like Christa and Andrew, and they desire larger roles, like most actors, but I don't see them as murderers."

"Why? Because they're homosexuals? Weren't Leopold and Loeb gay?"

She hit his shoulder playfully. "Don't forget your girlfriend Cindi who seemed quite disappointed when relegated back to the throes of makeup and hair."

"Who would Cindi be partnered with?"

Jana grinned. "True. You seem to be the only man for Cindi, and I don't peg you for a murderer."

"Thanks. Right back at you." He snapped his thick fingers. "How about that Jason guy? He seems to always be hanging around Christa. No offense, but could he and Missy—?"

"They had an argument. I doubt Missy and Jason are plotting to do much of anything, except get each other's goat."

"Maybe that's what this is all about."

"What do you mean?"

"There were three unsuccessful attempts at murdering Christa. What if the attacker doesn't want Christa dead? What if he, or she, wants to kill everyone Christa loves to scare Christa into submission?"

"And we're back to Andrew Bianca, Christa's knight in shining armor."

Bove nodded. "Break time." He rose and dove into the pool. Once he completed a few laps, Bove climbed out of the pool and stood in front of Jana's chaise with water droplets cascading down his muscular body. "I'm heading to the cottage to change for Nick's wake. Want to be my date?"

Jana rose and handed him a towel from the cabana. "Isn't Cindi going?"

"Probably." He wrapped the towel around his broad shoulders. "But I'd rather go with my best girl."

Jana walked to the hot tub, and put on her cape. "Better not let Cindi hear you say that or there might be another murder on set."

"Jana Lane can take care of herself. I'll pick you up in a half hour." He took a few steps then stopped and turned toward her. "Jana, whatever it is that's upset you, I'm right there with you whenever you're ready to tell me."

She sighed. "I don't mean to be evasive."

"It's killing me that something's bothering you." He stood next to her.

"I know. I'll tell you about it soon."

"I'm on your side. Always. Don't forget that."

She squeezed his shoulder. "I won't."

As the sun turned into a golden shaft of light with outstretched arms of indigo, violet, cherry, and tangerine, Jana went back into the house, up the spiral staircase, and peeked in on B.J. Then she reapplied her makeup, teased her hair, and changed into a taupe chiffon dress with matching pumps, shawl, and purse.

Bove honked his horn, and Jana flew down the stairs to join him. During the brief drive to the local funeral home, Jana couldn't help notice how dapper Bove looked in his black suit with his hair slicked back.

Upon entering, they were directed by a grave-looking man in a black suit to the parlor off the hallway. The room was furnished with easy chairs, loveseats, and wingback chairs in clusters facing the casket at the front. Christa and Andrew stood next to the casket receiving condolences from the visitors who appeared to be mostly past and present colleagues of Nicholas Hartford's. Christa wore a rayon black dress, and as usual Andrew was in a dark suit that hung off his thin body. When it was Jana and Bove's turn to offer their regrets, Andrew thanked Jana and Bove for attending then quickly led Christa away.

Jana spotted Karen Evans, in a black leather off-the-shoulder blouse and skirt, and Herm Fenton, in a black turtleneck and chinos, sitting on a loveseat at the opposite side of the room. The two gay couples, wearing stylish dark suits, shared a large sofa toward the back of the room. Jason Franks, in a dark blue suit that looked as if it belonged to his father, sat in an easy chair facing Christa. He stood and asked Jana, "Is Missy coming?"

Jana offered him an understanding smile. "She's watching B.J."

He nodded and went back to his seat.

Cindi, in a low-cut black cocktail dress, touched Bove's arm, then asked Jana, "Do you mind if I steal this handsome man? I want to thank him again for arranging my acting debut." She frowned. "Even if it was only my five minutes of fame."

Karen joined them. "Moving from me to Cindi so soon, Bove?"

"Not soon enough." Bove turned to Jana. "Excuse us." Bove led Cindi to a loveseat next to the brick fireplace.

Karen grinned at Jana. "I enjoyed our scene today."

Not relishing the thought, Jana replied, "We have another one tomorrow."

"Yes, the big scene where you corner me into confessing." Karen unleashed her molars. "Better be on your game, Jana. I plan to do whatever is necessary to be convincing as a murderer."

That won't be too difficult. "I look forward to it. Excuse me." Jana walked to the rear of the room and sat in an easy chair across from the sofa. "Don't you four look lovely? I wish we were meeting under happier circumstances."

The two couples appeared as if children with a secret.

Jana added, "Actually, I'm surprised to see you here."

"Why is that?" Hyo asked.

Jana replied, "I know you aren't fond of Christa and Andrew."

"Can you blame us?" Alaster asked.

Jana leaned forward in her seat. "You could turn the other cheek."

"And get slapped twice?" Aisha replied. "As other minority groups have done in the past, someday gay people will unite and fight the discrimination and persecution from people like the Biancas." Her eyes filled with anger. "Until that day, all we can do is wait and watch."

"Nick concealed his sexual orientation for his entire life to get ahead in his career," Hyo said. "But the joke was on him. Nick told me his frustrated clandestine lovers abandoned him, and so did his career."

Alaster added, "And according to Nick, the niece who idolized him never once asked him about his personal life."

"Jana, can I talk to you?"

"Excuse me." Jana followed Christa to a corner of the room, next to an easel displaying pictures of Nicholas Hartford starring in low budget B movies as a much younger man.

"I overheard what Alaster said to you." Christa gazed at the photographs of her uncle and wiped a tear from her cheek. "He was such a handsome man. So talented and charismatic. I didn't ask Uncle Nick about his personal life, because it didn't matter to me."

Or so you wouldn't have to face the truth about the sexual orientation of the uncle you adored.

Christa sighed. "It's not true what they said. I may not approve of their lifestyle due to my religious beliefs, but I don't hate homosexuals."

Jana tented her fingers. "Christa, how would you have felt if when you told Nick about your engagement to Andrew, Nick had said *your* love was a sin?"

A crevice formed between Christa's eyebrows. "I don't know. I hadn't thought about it like that."

"Well, think about it, Christa. Gay people are our families, friends, neighbors, and co-workers—especially in show business."

"I just don't understand why good and decent people make that choice."

"Being gay isn't a choice, but being homophobic is."

Christa shivered. "Andrew will never accept homosexuals."

"But you aren't Andrew. You're *you*." Jana smiled. "And the you I've gotten to know this week seems like she has enough love and understanding in her to welcome everyone."

"You are such a good friend." Christa wrapped her arms around Jana, and they shared a long hug. Then Christa gasped. "I'm so sorry. My makeup ran onto your dress!"

Jana looked down at the spot of blue eye shadow on her shoulder. "No problem."

"I don't want your dress to be ruined. Please, go to the ladies' room and wipe it before Reverend Walter comes to do the eulogy and prayer."

"All right." Jana left the parlor. She noticed two smaller parlors on the opposite side of the main hallway. Though the door was closed and the lights were off, she heard voices coming from the south parlor. The voices sounded very much like Andrew's and Karen's. Jana tiptoed to the doorway and listened in the shadows.

Karen said, "I didn't know you were interested in my soul, Andrew."

He replied, "I am *very* interested."

"Good, because I definitely need to be saved."

"And I'm the man to help you with that."

Karen giggled and cooed. "It looks like my soul is in your hands. Among other things."

Andrew chortled wickedly. "Would you like to…pray together?"

"Definitely. My…hallelujahs will raise you up faster than the Rapture and higher than Heaven."

Andrew replied with a shaky voice, "Praise the Lord!"

"But we need to form a covenant first."

"Like Abraham did with God?"

"Yes, but this one's just a little different."

Jana heard papers rustling.

Karen said, "Sign right there."

"What am I signing?"

"A contract for Karen Evans to star in Nevgere's next production."

Andrew gasped. "I can't do that."

"Then I can't get down on my knees and...repent."

"You drive a hard bargain."

"You have no idea."

They laughed.

I can't listen to any more of this! Following the sign in the lobby, she went down the stairs to the lower level and walked down the hallway, spotting the sign for the ladies' room at the end of the long corridor. Suddenly, she heard heavy breathing. She looked behind her and saw nobody. She kept walking with the distinct feeling that someone was following her. Jana picked up the pace and hurried into the ladies' room. Once she finished cleaning her dress, she tried the door. It didn't open. She pulled harder. It was sealed shut. She pounded on the door. Nothing. Jana cried out and kicked the door. Still nothing. Suddenly the door opened. She slowly entered the hallway then walked toward the stairs. *Somebody is watching me. I can feel it in every nerve of my body.* Jana walked faster and reached for the bannister. At the first step, she lost her footing and fell into the strong arms of Chris Bove.

"I wondered what happened to you. Are you all right?"

Jana took in some much needed air and was surrounded by the scent of pine. "It seems I am when I'm with you."

Chapter 9

Bove dropped Jana off at her mansion, where she checked in on B.J., washed and put on a gold satin nightgown, then lay on the chaise in her bedroom and phoned Brian. "How's the mall magnet?"

"Feeling like he's been mauled by politicians, environmental groups, store owners, and pretty much everyone else in Florida."

"Even the famous mouse?"

"Very funny."

"Any word from Dr. Borress?"

"Not yet."

"You hanging in?"

"That's a good way to describe it."

Brian replied, "We'll take things one step at a time. Everything will work out fine."

"That's what I keep telling myself." *Come home.* "When are you coming home?"

"Hopefully in a few days. Unless you need me sooner."

"I can't wait to see you."

He sighed. "I miss you and the boys like crazy, babe."

"We miss you, too." She lay back on the chaise. "Devon and Ed are fine."

"I know. I talked to them an hour ago."

"They're still up?"

"Probably hidden under the sheets with flashlights telling ghost stories for most of the night. Speaking of dead people, how's my wife, the famous sleuth?"

"Somebody threw Christa into the supply closet today."

"Is she alive?"

"Miraculously. I was walking down the hallway and must have scared them away."

"Jan, I thought you were going to be careful."

"I was careful."

"Walking into a storage closet with murderers? Where was B.J.?"

"With Missy and everyone else on set."

Brian sighed. "Figure this out soon before anything happens to you or B.J."

"Nothing has happened to us, except somebody is following me."

"What!"

"When I walked back from the cottage after Bove made me dinner, and tonight at Nick's wake."

Brian groaned. "I've given up fighting you on this, Jan. Sort through the suspects, think about your old movies, and tell Rivera, Bove, or whoever you're sleuthing with who did it."

"That's exactly what I intend to do."

"That's my girl."

While I finish shooting the TV pilot and hosting the AIDS gala at the park.

"Is Bove still hot for you?"

"He likes Cindi, our makeup woman who now plays Nurse One, formerly played by Bove's ex-wife Karen, a leather dominatrix who graduated to the role of the hospital administrator who is the murderer."

"You figured it out?"

"On the show, not in real life. Though Karen could certainly be the murderer due to jealousy. The same could be true of Cindi who seems to be hiding something about her past."

"Of course." Brian sighed.

"And I understand that Andrew gave Christa the money to enter the beauty pageant, but what does she see in him? He's a domineering, cheating husband."

"Unlike yours."

"And I can understand the gay couples being angry with Christa and Andrew, but if they tried to murder every homophobic person in the world, they would have a lot of blood on their hands."

Brian yawned.

"Get a good night's sleep."

"Impossible without my cuddle partner."

"She's waiting for you."

"That's my girl. They can't keep Jana Lane Otley down. We'll be together soon—and forever."

"Not soon enough, but definitely for forever. I love you."

Jana heard Brian's snoring. She hung up and made another call. "Reverend Heather, I'm sorry to bother you at night."

"It's never a bother to hear from you, Jana."

Jana filled in Reverend Heather on the events at the studio and her medical tests.

"It sounds like you've been facing your own Goliath, Jana."

"Actually, I've been feeling like Job."

"Don't we all from time to time? I wish you had told me about your appointment with Dr. Borress. I would have come with you."

"Thank you, but there isn't anything you could have done."

"I could have prayed. Just as I did when *I* went through it."

Jana gasped. "I didn't know that!"

"There's a lot about me that you and my other congregants don't know."

"Are you all right?"

"I'm always all right, because God is beside me. I didn't always feel all right, however, especially after the surgery and radiation treatments."

"But you are fine now?"

"Cancer free for ten years. More importantly, fear free."

Jana sat up straight on the chaise. "Reverend Heather, why do people face challenges?"

Reverend Heather sighed. "You mean why do bad things happen to good people?"

"I didn't mean to infer that I'm good."

"You're as good as good gets, Jana Lane Otley. As you know from my sermons, I don't believe God is the cause of wars, ill fortune, and disease. I believe God is heavenly spirit, there for the asking, ready to pick us up when we fall down, hold us up when our knees buckle, and cradle us on our last days. We just need to listen, have faith, and follow the path of love not fear. You're a wonderful woman who loves and is loved, defends those less fortunate, and works for justice for all. Hold onto that and never let it go." She said a prayer.

Jana thanked and said goodnight to Reverend Heather, climbed into bed, and sank into the silk white sheets.

****

Jana Lane ran down the white hospital hallway gasping for breath. As the footsteps behind her grew as loud as her heartbeat, she hurried into the supply closet and closed the door behind her. Afraid to make a sound, Jana hid behind the supply cabinet—until the door opened. Jana sprang up and raced out the rear door into an office then hurried back to the hallway— with her assailant's breath stinging her neck.

The next morning, Jana rose from bed soaking wet, again having spent much of the night lying awake. She showered, dressed in sweat clothes, and exercised in her home gym. When B.J. called for her from his bedroom, she helped him wash and dress then she hurried down the stairs with Missy following to meet the car to the studio.

Upon arriving at the old hospital, they ate breakfast in the main meeting room. Then Jana put Missy in charge of B.J., headed for her dressing room to change into her hospital patient attire, and sat in a chair in the makeshift makeup room. Looking at herself in the mirror, Jana hoped Cindi could make the bags under her eyes disappear.

Cindi teased Jana's hair in fans down her face. "What a shame about Stu and Nick."

Jana nodded without ruining her hairdo. "Did you get home all right last night?"

"Yes. Thank you for asking Bove to drive me home after he dropped you off."

I'll bet you invited him in for a nightcap. "You like Bove, don't you?"

Cindi giggled. "What woman wouldn't?"

Ask his exes.

"He's gorgeous, masculine, caring"—Cindi blushed—"and a good kisser."

No argument here. "Kudos again on your Nurse One scene."

Cindi picked up the base makeup. "It was only one scene."

"But it was a good one."

"And now I'm just the makeup girl." She applied the base to Jana's face.

"I'm sure you'll get to act again. I hope the acting exercise I gave you helped?"

"Exercise?"

"Thinking back to a time when you were scared about your past."

Cindi swallowed hard. "Yes, that helped."

Jana tried not to move her face as Cindi applied clown white under her eyes then rouge to her cheeks. "I don't mean to pry, but whatever you were thinking about seemed to upset you. I hope you aren't in any trouble."

"I hope not, too." Cindi blinked back tears.

"What is it, Cindi? Maybe I can help."

"Nobody can help me, Jana."

"Try me. Please." Jana noticed Cindi's hands shaking. "I won't let you put on my eye makeup unless you do."

Cindi wiped her eyes with a tissue and sat on the adjacent chair. "I'm originally from Philly. After high school I met a guy there. He owned the beauty parlor where I worked. He was a good deal older than me. He took me out in a plush car to fancy restaurants and bought me expensive gifts. My parents nearly had a stroke. We dated for six months then he had a heart attack and passed away. I was brokenhearted. My folks were thrilled. To my surprise, he left me the shop in his will. I was ecstatic. Not due to greed, but for the knowledge that I'd always have something that was his." A grave look came over her pretty face. "Unfortunately, his 'business associates' didn't see it that way. Three men in dark suits came to see me one day at the beauty parlor. They said he owed them a lot of money, so the shop was theirs. They made it quite clear that I needed to get out of town fast. And that's exactly what I did. Right after I sold the shop and hid the check in my suitcase."

"Where did you go?"

"I drove from one sleepy little town in Pennsylvania to the next, praying the men wouldn't find me. Eventually I landed here. Thinking Hyde Park, New York was far enough away from Philly, I used the money I had left to buy a beauty parlor." She rose and applied eyeliner.

With Jana's eyes closed, she asked, "Cindi, when you were driving around Pennsylvania, did you stay in a mountain town called Renovo?"

Cindi applied the eye shadow. "I don't recall. I drove through so many places."

"Did you meet Christa or Andrew when you were in Pennsylvania?"

"I don't believe so." She applied the mascara then looked at Jana in the mirror. "Perfect. I'll see you on set."

Jana held her arm. "Cindi, are you afraid these men might still find you?"

Cindi nodded. "It keeps me up at night."

"And no doubt dating an ex-detective would make

you feel more comfortable."

She leaned over Jana. "But that's not why I like Bove. He's a terrific guy. Handsome, strong, smart, honest." She smiled in recollection. "And we both love great food. If he weren't in love with you, I think Bove and I would have a future together."

Jana gasped. "Bove isn't in love with me."

Cindi patted her shoulder. "Dream on, girl. That man is smitten with you big time—and with your son. I've noticed the way he looks at you, talks to you, and worries about you."

"But I'm married—happily. And B.J. loves his father. His *real* father."

"Which is what I keep holding onto."

"How's my baby doll this morning?" Simon stood in the doorway wearing a lemon and lime swirled jumpsuit, cerise scarf, and lavender fanny pack. "Ready for the last day of shooting on the pilot?"

"Ready as I'll ever be to face the showdown with Karen."

As Jana rose from the chair, Cindi said, "Excuse me, Simon. I don't mean to bother you or to be pushy and obnoxious. And I'm sure you've heard this a million times from every wannabe actress in New York. But I was thinking…I mean it's just a thought—"

"My roster of actresses is more than full with the one and only Jana Lane." Simon put his small arm around Jana and led her out of the makeup room.

As they walked down the hallway behind the squawking walkie-talkie, Jana said to Simon, "Cindi's a nice girl."

"But she's no Jana Lane."

Jana smiled. "Is everything ready for the gala at the

park tonight?"

He nodded proudly. "Cornelius and I have everything under control." Simon glared at her. "Despite the short time to prepare."

She kissed his cheek.

They arrived at the hallway set up with lights, cameras, microphones, a track on the floor, and various technicians racing around them. Karen stood at the end of the hallway in a plum business suit, staring at Jana as if a prizefighter heading to meet her opponent in the ring. Herm walked and talked them through the scene beginning in Karen's office. Jana confronts Karen with what she has figured out, honing in on Karen as the organ launderer and murderer. Karen chases Jana down the hallway. Upon reaching the end of the hall, Karen reaches for Jana's throat. Using a move from *The Pirate Princess*, Jana hurls the side of her foot into Karen's knee, sending Karen to the ground. Bove arrives and handcuffs Karen.

A number of rehearsals were needed to synchronize the various technical elements of the scene. Jana had learned from past experience to mark the action during rehearsals and save her energy for shooting. Karen seemed to understand and follow the same pattern.

Herm finally called, "Quiet on the set!"

Cindi freshened their makeup.

The director yelled, "Roll camera! Slate! Action!"

Jana and Karen played their verbal sparring scene in Karen's office with excitement and high energy. Karen's denial of the facts ignited Jana to hurl more accusations against the hospital administrator. When it was clear that Jana would not keep quiet about what she had uncovered, Karen clenched her fists.

When Herm was satisfied with the various shots and angles, they continued on to the latter part of the scene extending down the hallway. "Roll! Slate! Action!"

Karen sprang like a tiger. Jana literally ran for her life. Reminiscent of her dreams, Jana raced down the hallway with her attacker at her heels. She felt her assailant's warm breath and sensed her outstretched hands. Not knowing if she was awake or asleep, Jana continued running down the hospital hallway with her heart pounding in her ears and sweat dripping down her back. When she reached the end of the hallway, Karen grabbed Jana hard by the throat. When Jana extended the side of her foot, Karen was ready for her. She grabbed it and pulled until Jana hit the ground. Jana remembered another move from the same movie, where the pirate king attacked her. As Karen dove at her, Jana placed her elbow in front of her face, which landed at Karen's neck. Karen fell to her side and lay stunned on the floor. Bove entered and took out his handcuffs.

"Cut! Check the gate! We got it in one take!" Herm helped Karen up and congratulated her on a job well done as they walked down the hallway.

Bove assisted Jana in rising to her feet. "Are you all right?"

"I am now that I know I'll never have to work with Karen Evans again. That woman is dangerous." They walked down the hallway. "How did you live with that woman?"

"It wasn't easy."

"Cindi seems much more your type."

"You're my type."

"Obviously not since I'm happily married." She couldn't resist. "And since I heard you and Cindi shared a little love next to the lamppost last night."

"It was just a little kiss."

"Not to Cindi. That girl is smitten."

The wardrobe woman waved down Jana and asked her to change into the same sweater and slacks she wore for her first scene. Once she had done so, she left her dressing room, happy to be out of her hospital garb.

As she waited to be called onto the set, Jana sat on the window seat in the main meeting room and played a game of checkers with B.J. Sitting across from them on an easy chair, Missy suddenly grew pale. Sweat lined the young woman's forehead, and her breathing became labored.

Jana asked, "Missy, what's wrong?"

"I feel weak…and a bit dizzy."

"You should go to the hospital."

Jason was at Missy's side in a flash. "I'll drive her. It's only a few minutes away."

"You don't have to do that." Missy blinked then blinked again.

Jana asked, "What's wrong with your eyes?"

"I see black spots in front of them."

Jana nodded to Jason who took Missy by the hand and led her to the doorway. He shouted over his shoulder, "I'll call from the hospital."

"Thank you, Jason." Jana looked after them, praying Missy would be all right.

B.J. asked, "What's wrong with Missy?"

Jana fabricated a smile. "Missy has a tummy ache. Jason is taking her to see the doctor. I'm sure Missy will be fine."

"Clownie and I don't like tummy aches."

A production assistant appeared. "I need to take B.J. to wardrobe for his last scene."

B.J. grinned from ear to ear. "To the camera?"

Jana explained, "First you have to change clothes."

The production assistant said over his squawking walkie-talkie, "I'll bring him back when he's finished."

"Thank you."

B.J. held onto Clownie, and the production assistant led him out of the room.

Christa appeared and sat next to Jana on the window seat. "B.J.'s quite a boy."

Jana smiled at Christa. "And you are quite a woman."

"What did *I* do?"

"You lost your agent and the uncle you long admired. Three attempts were made on your life, and you kept on shooting this week without any complaints or requests for concessions."

Christa looked over at Officer Lesar standing in the corner of the room watching her. "Between Andrew, Officer Lesar, and you, I feel protected."

That's my cue. "Christa, I don't want to gossip, but I overheard Andrew speaking with Karen at the funeral last night." Jana squirmed in her seat. "They were in one of the other parlors…with the door shut. It sounded as if they were…getting friendly."

"That doesn't surprise me. Andrew is a very friendly person."

Reload. "I mean, before I left to go to the bathroom, it sounded as if Andrew and Karen were becoming…intimate."

Christa giggled. "Jana, you don't come from an

evangelical background. We lay hands on people, pray for them, hug them, cry with them, and care deeply for their souls. Andrew is on fire for the Lord. He loves nothing more than to share the spirit with people."

He was sharing something all right. "Karen asked Andrew to sign a contract."

"It must be for Nevgere Productions. I have no head for legal issues. I'm lucky to have Andrew taking care of all that."

"Christa, it seemed like Karen was stating a demand—for services rendered."

"What kind of services?"

Jana swallowed hard. "Sexual favors for a role in Nevgere's next production."

Christa waved Jana away. "Why would anyone sign a contract for that? I'm sure it was a business discussion about hiring Karen for an upcoming project. She was quite good in her scenes with you. Andrew told me how impressed he was with her talents."

He was impressed with Karen's talents all right. "Christa, please speak to Andrew. I hate to tell you this, but I strongly suspect he may be carrying on with other women."

"Andrew would never commit the sin of adultery." Christa looked deeply into her eyes. "Jana, believe me when I tell you that if I'm sure of nothing else in this world, I am sure of Andrew's absolute love and devotion for me. I'd risk my life on it."

You may be doing just that. "Where is Andrew now?"

"On the phone in the hallway, discussing my next film role with the studio."

So much for Andrew staying at Christa's side. Jana

was happy for her new friend. "What will you be playing?"

"A stewardess who time travels. Andrew thinks with *Back to the Future* being such a big hit, this is the script I should take. Nevgere Productions will produce."

"Were you offered other film roles as well?"

Christa nodded. "Five." She giggled. "Including playing Madame Curie."

"You'd make a wonderful Madame Curie."

"Andrew likes the time travel script better."

Jana hugged her. "Congratulations, Christa. You are certainly on your way."

Tears filled Christa's eyes. "I wish Stu and Uncle Nick could be here to see it."

"I'm sure they're proud of you, Christa."

"Maybe not so proud." Christa looked out the window.

Jana rested a hand on her shoulder. "Christa, during a couple of our conversations, you mentioned 'mistakes' you've made. You've also mentioned Stu getting your career on the right track. I can't help but wonder what you are referring to."

Christa looked around the room then whispered, "I'm not proud of this, Jana."

"What is it, Christa? I promise, I won't judge you."

"I know you won't." Christa's face was wracked with pain. "My senior year in high school, after my parents had died and I was left taking care of my younger sisters and brother, a neighbor who knew I was in trouble offered me some money."

"Money for what?"

Christa wiped her eyes with a tissue. "To pose for

pictures."

Oh, Christa. "I understand."

"No, I don't think you do. I was desperate. I had nowhere else to turn. So I let go of my pride—and my clothing—and I made those disgusting poses as instructed. Andrew doesn't know about it. Nobody does. Well, Stu knew, thankfully."

"How did Stu find out?"

"After I won the beauty pageant and Stu took me on as his client, the photographer heard about it and wanted money not to publish the pictures. Stu, bless him, paid him off in exchange for the negatives." Christa wept. "Please don't think badly of me, Jana. I wouldn't blame you if you did, but I couldn't bear it."

"I wouldn't. I don't." She took Christa's hand. "You were the victim, Christa. That man took advantage of your situation."

"Stu Silverman saved me then, and he saved me when that light screen came toward me on the set. And now he's gone." Christa wept on Jana's shoulder.

Jana took Christa by the shoulders and wiped her eyes with a tissue. "That is all in the past. And the past is done and finished. Today is a new day. And you are a gorgeous, young, talented actress with a loving husband. And you received five film offers!"

Christa smiled. "More importantly, I'm someone who has made a wonderful and supportive new friend in the movie star she has long idolized: Jana Lane."

"And tonight you are going to attend my gala benefit at Bowdoin Park and eat, drink, dance, and celebrate the wrap of the TV pilot, while donating money to a worthwhile charity."

A production assistant led the two couples out of

the main meeting room and onto the set.

Christa looked after them. "I thought hard on what you said about…people like Uncle Nick, Simon, Hyo, Alaster, Siobhan, and Aisha."

"And?"

Christa held Jana's hand. "Everybody has the right to be as God created them. If God can love me the way I am, I should be like God and love others, too."

Jana wrapped her arms around Christa and hugged the woman to her chest. "I'm so proud of you, Christa."

A production assistant interrupted them. The young woman lowered the volume on her squawking walkie-talkie. "Excuse me, Jana, we got a call from Jason Franks. Your nanny is getting tests done in the hospital and feeling better."

Jana breathed a sigh of relief. "Thank you for letting me know."

Herm entered the room and called, "Lunch!"

The production assistant rushed over to Herm. "Jason Franks said he set all the props for the rest of the scenes before he left."

Herm picked at a pockmark on his nose. "Where'd he go?"

Jana rose. "I asked Jason to accompany my son's nanny to the hospital during her medical emergency."

Herm said to the production assistant, "Tell him to come back as soon as he can. Where's Karen Evans?"

No doubt starting a new career as a woman wrestler.

The production assistant blushed. "She said she's waiting to eat lunch with you in the solarium."

Herm smiled and headed for the lunch table, where he quickly filled two plates, then left the meeting room.

Jana thought about phoning Dr. Borress and her hands began to shake, realizing that one phone call could change her entire life.

B.J. returned with another production assistant, and Andrew entered shortly thereafter. While Jana, B.J., Christa, and Andrew ate lunch, Jana noticed the gay couples watching them from the opposite side of the room. Jana asked Christa to watch B.J., then she walked over to them. "Would you like to join us?"

Hyo did a double-take. "I don't think Christa and Andrew would like that."

"You might be surprised"—Jana smiled—"at least about Christa."

"I doubt it," Alaster replied.

Jana said, "Well, if you change your mind."

Aisha stood and took Jana's hand. "Thank you."

"For what?" Jana asked.

Siobhan replied, "For standing up for us here, and giving us the touring jobs."

Bove tapped Jana on the shoulder. "Can we talk?"

"Sure." Jana walked Bove to the window seat.

Once they were seated, he said, "Are you okay?"

"I'm fine."

"You don't look fine. What did you eat for lunch?"

"Yogurt and fruit."

"That's not enough."

"Is that what you wanted to talk about?"

He shook his head then looked at the floor. "I was wondering…Cindi asked me…if it's not all right I'll understand…the issue is—"

"Lunch is nearly over, Bove. Spit it out."

He blurted out, "Is it okay if I take Cindi to the AIDS benefit tonight?"

She laughed. "You don't need my permission to go out on a date, Bove."

"I know. I assumed…that you assumed…the assumption that you and I would assumedly…"

Jana squeezed his knee. "Enjoy your date with Cindi. I'm pleased you're both coming to the benefit."

"You're not jealous?"

"Not at all." *Maybe if I repeat that three times fast, I'll actually believe it.*

He kissed her cheek then hurried back to Cindi.

Jana checked her watch. *It's now or never.* She rose on shaky legs and headed for the pay phone in the hall. As she lifted the receiver, her hands shook out of control. Christa came out of the ladies' room and flew to Jana's side. "What's wrong?"

"With all you're going through, I don't want to bother you with this."

Christa said, "I've been leaning on your shoulders throughout this whole week. Now it's my turn to offer mine. They aren't as strong as yours, but they're there for you, girlfriend."

Jana couldn't deny she was happy her new friend was by her side. "I have to phone my doctor for some test results."

Christa hung up the phone and walked Jana to a window seat. Once they were seated, Christa put her arm around Jana. "First let's pray." Christa asked God to watch over her good friend, give her courage and patience, and provide a good outcome.

Then Christa walked Jana back to the phone and held her hand as Jana made the call. Jana thought about Brian and the boys as she gave her name to the receptionist. Suddenly a feeling of calm came over her.

Whatever the result or the prescribed treatment plan, she was ready to face it and come out victorious.

"Jana, it's Dr. Borress."

"Hello, Dr. Boress," Jana replied with a quivering voice.

"The news is good. All the tests came back negative. Your lump is probably just a cyst. Make an appointment to come see me again and we'll investigate further."

Jana didn't hear the rest of what the doctor said to her. She hung up the phone and wept in Christa's arms.

"Bad news?" Christa asked.

Jana hugged her new friend. "Good news. Very good news."

Christa kissed her cheek.

Holding Christa's hand, Jana phoned Brian. "I spoke to Dr. Borress. I'm all right, honey."

"I'm so relieved, babe."

"Me, too."

"I told you nothing could bring Jana Lane Otley down."

"I love you, Brian."

"Right back at you, Jan. Forever and ever."

Jana hung up the phone and wiped her eyes. "Thank you, Christa."

Christa put an arm around her. "What are friends for?"

The assistant director called lunch over. A production assistant led Jana, B.J., Bove, Cindi, and Christa down the hallway with Officer Lesar, Andrew, and Simon following close behind. They stopped at the room set up as the nurse's station. Another production assistant led Hyo, Alaster, Aisha, and Siobhan into the same room.

For the last scene in the episode, Jana was reunited with her husband and son. Then she said goodbye to the grateful hospital staff she saved from the hospital administrator. Jana's last goodbye was for the nurse she had befriended.

They rehearsed the scene then Cindi touched up their makeup, spending extra time on Bove. Herm called for "Roll! Slate! Action!" and they filmed the long shot. It was an easy acting assignment for Jana to be excited about seeing Bove and B.J. Again B.J. ad libbed a request for Jana to kiss Clownie, too. It was also true to life for Jana to tell Hyo, Alaster, Aisha, and Siobhan how pleased she was to have met them, and to wish them well in the future. When it came time for Jana to say goodbye to Christa, Jana was surprised when tears rolled down her cheeks. As in the script, Jana had grown quite close to Christa, and while she was happy for Christa's success, she would miss her new young friend a great deal. With Jana and Christa weeping in each other's arms, Herm shouted, "Cut! Let's move on to the close-ups!"

Given the number of cast members, they had to do the scene numerous times. Each take Jana felt just as sad to be leaving her new little family, especially Christa, and Cindi had to repair Jana's and Christa's makeup.

Herm shouted, "Cut! It's a wrap!" and everyone cheered. "No wrap party since we'll all be at the park benefit tonight. Crew, you're on early tomorrow morning for pack up and clean up." He shouted at a production assistant. "Tell Jason when he gets back." Then he hollered to the rafters, "Thanks, everybody.

The pilot is going to be terrific!"

When the applause ended, Simon said, "And I would like to offer a special thank you and congratulations to the star of our show, Jana Lane, who, as usual, was the perfect role model for everyone." Riding the applause, he added, "And after only one week off, the crew will be re-joining Jana, Bove, and B.J. for episode two of *The Detective's Wife*."

Week off? I'll be memorizing another hundred pages of dialogue. Jana addressed the crowd. "I would like to thank everyone for being so professional, friendly, and hardworking in these extremely difficult circumstances. Each one of you is to be commended for your unwavering dedication." She took Christa's hand. "But most of all, I want to thank the true hero of our company. The woman who stood strong through the most harrowing of experiences and great personal loss, and never missed a beat. My new friend who stood by me when I needed her. Christa, I know your star is shooting across the sky. But I'm honored that you passed by the set of *The Detective's Wife* on your way. Please know you will always have a place here to come back and visit. And you will truly be missed."

Christa replied, "Jana, you're right. I lost a great deal this week. And I dedicate my performance to Stu Silverman and Nicholas Hartford. But I gained a great deal, too. My childhood idol is now my close friend." As everyone applauded, Christa wept on Jana's chest.

Wrapping his thin arm around his wife's shoulder, Andrew led Christa away. "Let's get you back to the hotel so we can talk about your upcoming film project, honey."

As the crowd dispersed, Bove tapped Jana's

shoulder. "You did good."

Jana looked up into his sparkling emerald eyes. "You, too, partner."

"Everything okay with what was bothering you?"

She smiled. "Everything is very okay."

He wrapped his arms around her and they shared a long hug.

"Bove, just think, if the show's a hit, we may be doing this until we're old and feeble."

Bove held her hand. "I'd be honored to be your husband...on camera for as long as you'll have me."

"Where is the camera going, Mommy?"

Jana put her arm around her son. "The camera needs a rest, but it will be back." She turned to Bove. "Can you please do me a favor? Take B.J. home, and ask Theresa to look after him until I get there?"

"Sure," Bove replied. "What's up?"

"I'm going to ask a production assistant to drive me to the hospital to see Missy."

"You got it."

A few minutes later, Jana was in a real hospital. Upon making her way through the various floors and corridors, she entered Missy's room and found Jason sitting by Missy's side. "How's the patient?"

Missy blushed. "My blood work was fine except for low blood sugar."

"So for now, all we have to do is make sure Missy eats regularly," Jason explained. "Then there should be no more dizzy spells."

Jana plopped into the other chair. "Thank goodness."

"They're releasing me soon," Missy said.

Jason smiled. "And I'm taking her to your benefit

dinner tonight."

"Make sure she eats something," Jana said. She held Missy's hand. "You have to take care of yourself, Missy. It's very important, now more than ever."

"Don't worry, Jana. I'm on it." Jason took Missy's other hand.

Jana winked at him. "You're a good guy, Jason."

Missy nodded. "I found that out."

"Don't forget it." Jana turned to Jason. "Are you taking Missy home?"

"I sure am," he replied.

"Good. Right after you do, be sure to stop by the studio and check in with Herm."

"Will do." Jason asked, "How did shooting go?"

"Fine. We're wrapped. For this episode anyway."

"Let's hope there are many more." Jason looked at Missy with adoration in his eyes. "So I'll have lots more time to see Missy on the set."

Missy sat up in bed. "You'll be seeing me more than on the set." She looked at Jana sheepishly. "If that's okay with you, Jana?"

"It's *more* than okay with me." Jana looked at her watch. "I need to go home and get changed. I'll ask Theresa to work late and take care of B.J. tonight, so you can stay as late as you like at the benefit."

Jason squeezed Missy's hand. "That sounds like fun."

Missy giggled and blushed.

Jana left the hospital and the driver took her home. Since Theresa's nighttime soap operas were on that evening, Theresa agreed to stay and watch B.J. Jana read B.J. a story, got his dinner, and washed and dressed him for bed. Then she smothered her son with kisses and tucked him into bed. Next, she hurried across the hall to her bedroom and phoned Devon and Ed who seemed thrilled by the prospect of their upcoming overnight in a tent at the lake. When she gave Jackson her good news, he nearly hit the roof. Remembering, she phoned Dr. Borress' office to make her next appointment. Then calling Simon, she asked if he and Cornelius could escort her to the park that evening—in their car rather than on their motorcycle. Finally, she freshened up her makeup, arranged her hair in side waves with a bun at her neck then changed into a platinum satin strapless gown with matching necklace, shoes, and purse. She added the finishing touch of platinum eye shadow as the doorbell rang.

Moments later, Jana opened the large wooden front door to Simon in an electric crimson jumpsuit with a persimmon scarf and pistachio waist pouch. Cornelius hovered over his lover in a white tuxedo with an electric crimson handkerchief in his suit pocket, persimmon suspenders, and pistachio cummerbund. "You two look good enough to eat."

Simon kissed the air around Jana's face. "I don't want to ruin the makeup—yours or *mine*."

"You look smashing!" Cornelius said.

"Thank you." Jana spun in a circle.

Simon waved a finger at her. "But you let Bove get away. That makeup woman has her blood red nails all over him."

Jana turned to Cornelius. "How do you stand him?"

Cornelius replied, "Since I'm so much taller, most of the time I sit down."

They drove the short distance to Bowdoin Park, and Cornelius parked the car in the flagged off area for benefit guests.

Jana got out of the car and swooned. "A perfect warm evening for an outdoor event. And everything looks so beautiful!" She looked at the park's wooden pavilions decorated with huge red ribbons, red lanterns, and red balloons. Jana felt revived and renewed, as if she could conquer the world.

They walked on the Kelley-green lawn up the short hill to the first pavilion and gazed at the violet, vermilion, and peach sky caressing the mountains. Simon neatly arranged the brochures and pamphlets on the tables.

When they arrived at the second pavilion, Cornelius checked in with the musicians who were in their black tuxedos and gowns, tuning their instruments. Jana shook hands with each musician and thanked him or her for the generous donation of time and talent.

Leaving Cornelius with his orchestra, Jana and Simon walked the short distance to the third pavilion and admired the polished wooden dance floor. At the fourth pavilion, Jana's stomach growled at the sight and smells of the buffet tables loaded with sumptuous hot and cold appetizers, entrees, and desserts. Before Simon could taste each dish, Jana led him to the last and largest pavilion, which housed the tables and chairs for the guests, appointed with satin red tablecloths and gorgeous red rose crystal centerpieces. Jana's stomach dropped at the sight of the microphone set up at the front of the pavilion for her welcome speech.

The orchestra played as guests arrived and made their way from pavilion to pavilion. The wait staff served drinks to the guests already seated at their tables in pavilion five. Jana's heart leapt at the sight of

Reverend Heather and a number of her congregants at their table. "Reverend Heather, the tests came out okay."

Reverend Heather kissed her cheek. "I'm so proud of you for your bravery—and for your new foundation. We're announcing a special thank you to you and your foundation at this Sunday's service."

Jana hugged Reverend Heather and her congregants. "All of you coming tonight is thank you enough." She made her way from table to table welcoming and thanking those in attendance who each paid two hundred dollars for the worthy cause. Simon had worked his magic, so Jana thanked profusely a number of celebrities who had traveled from New York City for the event. When she got to the table of her colleagues from *The Detective's Wife*, Jana was happy to see Missy's cheeks matched her cherry-red dress. Jason, in a navy blue suit, was at Missy's side. Jana asked, "Are you feeling better, Missy?"

Missy held Jason's hand. "I am now."

Jason kissed Missy's cheek. "I'm going to make sure she stays that way."

Clad in a black leather, backless top and short leather skirt, Karen Evans' eyes narrowed. "Have you recuperated from our scene this morning, Jana?"

Herm picked at a pockmark on his chin. "I was really pleased with the finished product."

Jana smiled. "I was pleased when we were finished, too."

Jana noticed Christa in a pretty turquoise dress and matching cape. Andrew, as usual, wore a suit a few sizes too large for him. "Thank you both for coming," Jana said.

"Thank Christa, not me," Andrew said with a sneer.

Jana and Christa kissed cheeks. "Congratulations again, Christa. When do you leave to start your next film?"

Karen's face dropped. "What film is that?"

"Christa is playing a time traveling stewardess in a big studio film," Andrew said proudly. "Move over *Back to the Future*."

"And Christa received four other film offers!" Jana said.

Karen groaned.

A tad envious are we, Karen?

Some of the couples took to the dance floor in the dance pavilion. Jana noticed Hyo dancing with Aisha and Alaster dancing with Siobhan. She admired Hyo and Alaster's black tuxedos and Aisha and Siobhan's red gowns. At the conclusion of the song, *The Power of Love* by Huey Lewis and the News, Jana met them returning to their table in the last pavilion. "Don't you four look nice? Why aren't you dancing with your real partners?"

Hyo laughed bitterly. "I don't think that would go over too well. Even with this crowd."

Andrew pushed his glasses up his nose. "I'll tell you something. That food looks pretty good, but if I have to watch two guys dancing, I won't be able to keep it down."

Hyo's face tightened. "How is my dancing with Alaster about *you*, Andrew?"

"It's about me because I agreed to come to a dinner dance, not a homosexual bar."

Christa put her arm around her husband. "Would

you like to dance, honey?"

Andrew glared at Hyo and Alaster. "I did, until these guys started flaunting their lifestyle in my face."

Aisha leaned toward Andrew. "The only one flaunting anything is you flaunting your ignorance and bigotry."

"You're the one prejudiced against my religion," Andrew replied.

Christa rose. "Let's go to the food pavilion, honey."

"I think that's a good idea," Jana said.

Andrew didn't budge. "It's all in Leviticus."

"They have your favorites, Andrew: lobster and steak," Christa said, tugging at his arm.

Siobhan said, "And eating shellfish, like your shaved face, cut hair, and seventy-two other things are forbidden in Leviticus, Andrew."

Andrew rose and glared at them.

Not wanting a fight to break out at her event, Jana shot Christa a head nod toward the food pavilion.

Christa pulled Andrew away. "Let's enjoy the food, honey."

Jana smelled pine.

"May I have this dance?"

She gazed up at Bove, looking delicious in a powder blue T-shirt, white parachute pants, and white blazer. "Where's Cindi?"

"Looking at the brochures." He pointed to the first pavilion where Cindi, wearing a sunflower-colored cocktail dress, was leafing through the written materials about the Jana Lane AIDS Foundation. "I want the first dance with the hostess."

As the gay couples licked their wounds, Bove led

Jana to the dance pavilion. The orchestra played Simple Minds' "Don't Forget About Me." Bove took her in his strong arms and they danced.

Jana rested her head on his large shoulder. "Thank you for coming."

"I wouldn't miss it."

"You look great."

"So do you."

He looked down at her. "What's wrong now?"

"I'm nervous about giving my speech."

"You'll knock them dead as always." He smirked. "Bad choice of words."

"Speaking of which, did your girlfriend tell you the story about her past?"

"With the mobster who left her the beauty parlor?"

Jana nodded. "Cindi said she drove through most of Pennsylvania to dodge them. You think she might have hit Renovo in her travels and had a run-in with Christa?"

"Cindi never mentioned it."

"Neither did Christa."

Jana looked over at pavilion five. "Your ex-wife didn't seem happy about Christa's recent film offers."

"Karen isn't happy about too much."

"And Jason continues to watch Christa and Andrew with the oddest expression on his face."

"Has Christa remembered how she knows Jason?"

Jana shook her head. "And the two couples nearly came to blows with Andrew."

"That's not too hard to do. What does Christa see in that guy?"

"They say love is blind."

The song ended and Cornelius bowed toward Jana.

She and Bove walked back to pavilion five. "Wish me luck."

"Always."

Jana stood behind the microphone. "Can everyone please take your seat?" Once the guests were all seated, Jana looked from table to table. "It is with great honor that I announce to you the launch of the Jana Lane AIDS Foundation." During the applause, Jana noticed Andrew shaking his head from side to side. "Like many plagues in history, AIDS struck and struck hard. Unlike past medical crises, our representatives in government have been slow to offer their help and support. So it has been up to very few private organizations to fill that void. If any of you have been through a medical scare or crisis, you know how lonely, frightening, and debilitating it can be. We are setting the wheels in motion to change that." Jana spotted Andrew muttering, and Christa holding his hand. "Thanks to the skilled leadership of my longtime agent and friend, Simon Huckby"—Simon waved his napkin to the crowd—"my foundation has produced educational literature about this dreaded disease."

Andrew said loud enough to be heard, "Brainwashing propaganda."

The others at his table glared at him. Christa rested her cape on the back of her chair and whispered in his ear.

Jana ignored the interruption. "And every penny collected at benefits like this one will go toward research for a cure of this terrible disease, as well as financial and emotional support for its victims."

"The homosexuals."

A number of people shushed Andrew. Christa

cuddled with Andrew in what seemed like an attempt at keeping him quiet.

Jana didn't want to dignify his comment. "And we will soon be sending out a tour, where performers will share their talents and raise money all over the country. Four of those people are with us tonight." She pointed to her co-stars' table.

Andrew shouted to the crowd, "It's not me or my wife. Our Pastor Billy back home taught us traditional family values."

When the gay couples glared at Andrew, Christa switched seats with Andrew, sitting between Andrew and the two couples.

Aisha said, "To live off your wife's talent is really traditional, Andrew."

Andrew rose from his seat. Christa followed, holding onto his arm. Hyo and Alaster stood glaring at Andrew. Jana looked to Bove for help. He shrugged.

"Why not admit you're really collecting money for the homosexual agenda?" Andrew called out.

Reverend Heather rose and began singing the famous song, "We Are the World." Her congregants stood and joined in. The orchestra played, and the other guests followed along, holding hands and swaying back and forth to the tune of the music.

Jana exhaled as the singing drowned out Andrew's protests. When the song was finished, Jana said, "That is the spirit of the Jana Lane AIDS Foundation. Thank you all for sharing your spirit, compassion, generosity, and kindness. Now please help yourself to our sumptuous buffet."

The guests meandered to the food pavilion, filled their plates, and returned to their tables for dinner. Jana made her way from table to table making small talk, answering questions about her foundation, and once again thanking her guests for their donations.

Jana went back to her table and found Simon with three empty plates in front of him. "The food is delicious, baby doll. I think I'll help myself to another plate. Care to join me?"

"Sure."

Simon replied, "Careful, you don't want to put on any weight. The camera adds ten pounds."

Jana took Simon's small arm. As they made their way across the pavilion, she noticed the guests had finished eating and were milling around the tables. Suddenly, she heard a scream. Jana followed the sound to *The Detective's Wife* table. She made her way through the sea of guests and found Andrew slumped over the table with a knife in his back, and Christa crying out his name.

Chapter 10

Christa held out a knife full of blood. "Andrew!" She collapsed onto his back and wept, screaming his name over and over again.

Jana wrapped a napkin around the knife and placed it on the table.

Bove asked Cindi to use the park phone and call Rivera. Then he told everyone to move to the dance pavilion.

Jana lifted Christa to her feet and tried to lead her away from the table. Christa's eyes were wide and searching. "I can't leave Andrew."

"I know some first aid." Jason held Andrew's wrist. His face saddened. "I'm afraid he's gone."

"No! Andrew's not gone." Christa clutched at Jana's arm. "Andrew was sitting in *my* seat." She picked up a dinner knife. "Let them take me. Not Andrew. Not my Andrew. I can't live without my Andrew!"

Jana took the knife and placed it away from Christa on the table. Bove helped Jana move Christa to the next table with Christa screaming and reaching out. "Andrew! I want Andrew! It should have been me! He's not dead. He's not. Andrew!"

When Detective Rivera arrived, a female police officer brought Christa, kicking and screaming for Andrew, into the police car and they drove off. While

Bove spoke with Rivera and his other officers, Jana examined Andrew's body, noticing the bloody knife hole in his back.

Rivera came to her side. "I understand you have the murder weapon. Why doesn't that surprise me?" Jana pointed to the napkin on the table. Rivera bagged it. "What did you see?"

Jana replied, "When Andrew argued with some of the people at the table, Christa switched seats with him. After dinner everyone was milling around the table. I heard Christa scream,and looked back at Christa calling Andrew's name and pulling a knife out of Andrew's back. When I got to the table, she handed me the knife, and I wrapped it with the napkin."

"Jana didn't touch the knife." Bove was at her other side.

Rivera scratched his hair, unleashing a storm of dandruff onto the table. "Did either of you see who stabbed him?"

Jana and Bove shook their heads no.

Rivera walked Jana and Bove to the fourth pavilion. "My officers will tape off the crime scene, then get the guests' contact information after I question them. When I'm through, I'll go back to the station and interview Mrs. Bianca."

Jana said, "Christa needs a friend with her. I'd like to go to the station."

"And you may"—Rivera's eyebrows raised—"after *I* speak with her."

Rivera walked to the third pavilion. Jana followed and listened in on his interviews with her guests. Nobody had seen anything suspicious, except for Andrew's behavior.

When he was through, Rivera drove Jana to the police station. Jana waited outside Rivera's office as he questioned Christa. After a few minutes, Rivera asked Jana to join them. Jana and Christa sat opposite Rivera's white covered desk.

"The preliminary testing showed only Christa's fingerprints on the knife," Rivera explained.

Jana held Christa's hand. "Of course the killer would wear gloves. No doubt rubber gloves from the supply closet on our set."

Rivera turned to Christa. "Mrs. Bianca, can you please tell me what happened?"

Tears flowed down Christa's cheeks as she rocked back and forth. "I want my Andrew."

Rivera said to Jana, "That's all I could get out of her."

Jana squeezed her hand. "Please tell Detective Rivera what you know, Christa. Do it for Andrew, so we can catch his killer. I'll be right here next to you."

Finally Christa said, "It's my fault."

"It isn't your fault, Christa." Jana handed her a tissue. "Please tell us what happened."

Christa sucked in a deep breath. "I turned away from Andrew...to speak to Cindi. When I looked back at my husband...he was slumped over like that...with that knife in his back!" She wept on Jana's shoulder. "And he was in *my* chair!" She pulled away from Jana. "But I know Andrew isn't dead. He can't be. God wouldn't take Andrew away from me, Jana. You know that. Don't let them say Andrew is dead, Jana. Please! Don't let them!"

With Christa in a state of hysterics, Rivera called a doctor to give her a sedative and arranged for Christa to spend the night in the local hospital. Jana accompanied the police car to the hospital, and sat next to Christa's bedside, holding her hand.

Tears flowed down Christa's cheeks. After a few minutes, Christa turned to Jana. "Is Andrew really gone?"

Jana nodded. "I'm so sorry, Christa."

"I know people didn't like him, but they didn't know him like I did. We were childhood sweethearts. And he always treated me like a princess. Even at the benefit we were cuddling and cooing. I can't live without him, Jana. Why didn't they take me instead?"

Jana squeezed Christa's hand. "Get some rest. We'll talk more tomorrow, and figure out what to do next."

The second sedative administered by the nurse took effect. Christa said with slurred speech, "Andrew was...all I had...left." She clutched at Jana's hand. "Find out...who took him...from me."

"I promise you I will."

Then she fell asleep.

The police officer drove Jana home. Jana checked in on B.J., took off her clothes and makeup, washed, and put on her nightgown. She desperately wanted to talk to Brian, but she wouldn't wake him. Still concerned about Christa, she lay on her satin sheets and rested her head on her satin pillow.

Jana tossed and turned most of the night in a state of half-sleeplessness, thanking God for her test results, and remembering her promise to Christa. Her dreams of being chased down the hospital hallway were interspersed with memories of the last week: Stu saving Christa from the falling light screen. Stu eating poisonous herbs from the lunch plate. Nicholas Hartford tumbling down the staircase. Christa lying bleeding and unconscious on the supply closet floor. Andrew dead with a knife in his back in Christa's chair. Faces and snippets of things they had said filled her consciousness: Christa's account of her past poverty, verbal abuse, and desperation leading to the pictures with the photographer. Christa's idolization of her uncle. Stu Silverman's discovery of the young actress. Karen Evans' jealousy of Christa's rise to stardom and encounter with Christa's husband. The reaction of the two gay couples to Christa's initial parroting of her hometown homophobic Pastor Billy. Andrew owning Nevgere Productions. Cindi driving throughout Pennsylvania. Jason watching Christa and looking familiar to her. Brian entered her cognitions. "Sort through the clues and suspects and think about your old movies."

What happened to the missing rubber gloves and razor blade from the supply closet? Jana jumped up in bed. *I know the identity of the murderer!* She looked at the clock on her night table, which read six in the morning. *I need to get into that closet and make sure I'm right.* Knowing the film crew would be arriving at the old hospital set momentarily, Jana made a phone call. Then she washed, dressed in jeans and a sweatshirt, pulled her hair back in a ponytail, and left instructions with Missy to look after B.J. Finding B.J.'s Clownie rag doll on the hall floor, Jana picked it up, hurried into Devon's bedroom to retrieve his tape recorder, raced down the spiral staircase, and flew out the door.

Since there was little traffic so early in the

morning, Jana sped in her sports car to the old hospital parking lot. Upon entry into the building, she checked in with the technicians as they arrived to clean and close down the set.

Jana walked through the lobby to the main meeting room and finally to the hospital hallway. She sensed someone was following her. As in her dreams, Jana moved quickly down the hall. Hearing breathing, she walked faster. At the sound of footsteps behind her, Jana ran to the supply closet with her heart pounding like a drum. Sweat ran down her legs as she pulled aside Rivera's yellow tape and tried the door. It was locked.

"Looking for something?"

Jana spun around and faced Jason Franks. *Think fast, girl.* "Since it's clean-up day, I wanted to get something I had dropped in the supply closet set yesterday."

Jason looked quite different in a dress shirt, slacks, and blazer. "What did you drop?"

"My earrings."

"You weren't wearing earrings yesterday." He stood in front of the door. "You shouldn't be here."

"But *you* should." *It's now or never.* "And I know why."

Jason's shoulders dropped. "How did you figure it out?"

"I wondered why you kept watching all of us, especially Christa. I knew you weren't from this area when you used the term, 'pop' for soda."

He smiled. "I moved here a year ago."

"But not to work for Nevgere Productions."

"No."

Stay calm. "I wondered why Christa said she knew you from somewhere, but you were wearing different clothing."

"Of course I couldn't tell Christa where she had seen me," Jason said with a sense of maturity.

"That would have spoiled your cover."

"And I couldn't have that."

"No, you couldn't."

"How did you know?"

Jana smiled. "In my old movie *Surfer Girl*, my father played a police officer who posed as a lifeguard to keep an eye on me."

Jason ran a hand through his auburn locks. "Rivera nearly had my head when I told him Christa saw me in my police uniform when she arrived early the first day of shooting. I hadn't yet changed into my prop master clothes."

"Why did Rivera go through the trouble of getting you the job as prop master and stationing you at our film set—before any of the attacks?"

He imitated Rivera, "Because any time Mrs. Otley is involved in something, murder and mayhem will surely follow."

Thanks, Rivera.

"And Rivera hadn't heard of Nevgere Productions, and he wanted to make sure they were on the up and up."

"But you got involved with Missy, and that took your focus off your real job—watching for suspicious behavior."

"I felt terrible about that." His face lit up. "But I feel great about meeting Missy. How is she?"

"She was groggy but fine when I woke her up early

this morning."

Jason touched her arm. "I really like that girl, Jana."

"I'm glad, because that girl really likes you, too."

They shared a smile, then Jason tore down the yellow tape. "This can come down now." He unlocked the supply closet. "Feel free to look for whatever it is you 'lost.' I'll let the film crew clean up the other rooms while I report back to police headquarters—if I still have a job."

"Thank you, Jason, or should I say, Officer Franks."

"It's Officer Franklin. Please tell Missy I'll call her tonight and explain everything." He winked. "Good luck with your investigation."

When he was gone, Jana stepped into the storage closet. The blood and medical paraphernalia were gone, but the fallen cabinet still covered part of the floor. She walked past it to the standing supply cabinet. After placing Devon's tape recorder—with Clownie covering it—on top of the cabinet, she searched through the drawers finding nothing unusual, except the pack with the missing razor blade. Next, she examined the surrounding area. *The screen!* She inspected the white cloth screen covering the doorway into the office next door. On her knees, Jana grasped at the legs of the screen. *That's it!* She lifted one leg and pulled out a pair of balled up rubber gloves lodged inside one of the legs. She opened the gloves and found the razor blade—with caked on blood.

She heard the closet door close. Jana looked up at the face of the murderer.

"Don't try leaving through the other door. It's

locked. From the other side."

Jana rose and pushed down on Clownie's leg, turning on the tape recorder. "B.J. left Clownie in here. I came in to get him."

"I thought Jana Lane never lies. Give me the gloves and razor blade."

Jana handed them over.

"Like you, I was waiting for Jason to unlock the closet door."

"I know you've been following me all week, even outside my house and downstairs at Nick's funeral. And of course today in the hallway."

"And good thing, too. Now I realize I have to commit murder number four."

"How did you get out of the hospital, Christa?"

Christa Bianca smiled. "Miraculously, I was feeling better, and I just *had* to see the set where Andrew and I worked last." She winked at Jana. "One of the perks of being an actress."

Jana eyed the closet door.

"Don't think about getting past me. This country mountain girl is a lot stronger than *The Adorable Orphan*."

Keep her talking. "I know how you killed the others, Christa. How are you going to kill me?"

"The doctor at the hospital was nice enough to give me a prescription for sedatives." She opened her purse and held up the bottle. "I was always taught to share. So I'm going to share them—with you. *All* of them."

"Don't you want to know how I figured it out, Christa?"

"I know you're stalling, Jana. The film crew is busy loading lighting equipment into the van outside.

They won't be inside for quite some time." Christa sat on the downed supply cabinet. "So why not? Tell me how the great amateur detective, Jana Lane, figured everything out."

Jana took in a deep breath. "I remembered how Margaret in *School Spy* hid in the schoolyard, ripped her dress, and held her breath until she passed out. When the teacher found her, Margaret lied and said Timmy hit her and left her there."

"And Jana Lane figured out the truth and saved little Timmy. I remember. Jana, do you know why I asked Andrew to form Nevgere Productions and hire you as our star? I thought, if Jana Lane was on the set, nobody would be surprised when people were murdered. And if you couldn't find the truth, nobody could." She grimaced. "But you figured it out at the final reel." She sighed. "How?"

Jana cleared her throat. "You told me that you grew up very poor. The other children made fun of you and called you, 'Rag Doll.'"

Christa's eyes filled with tears. "You wouldn't know what it's like to be called names every day, pushed into a muddy road, laughed at. All the while knowing they were right. You were a poor, backwards, pathetic creature who nobody loved. And since I was unlovable, I decided I would never love anyone."

"But the other children underestimated you." Jana met Christa's eyes. "I learned in *The Littlest Farmer* that a rag doll is a breed of cat that collapses when picked up, but like all cats has sharp claws."

"Finish the first scene, Jana. Tell me what you know."

Stay focused and don't lose your cool. "But there

was a bright spot in your young life, your Uncle Nick, the great actor, who visited you from time to time with exaggerated tales of his wealth and fame. You mentioned asking him to assist you in following in his footsteps, and Nick not obliging. When your parents died, you asked your uncle again to take you with him. He gave you money to feed your brother and sisters, but not what you really wanted, a ticket out of Renovo."

Christa's face hardened. "And Uncle Nick didn't even come to my parents' funeral—because he was on a film shoot. I never forgave him for that."

"You were angry, poor, and desperate. As you confided in me, you agreed to pose naked for that photographer. You never told anyone else about it, not even Andrew who was in love with you and gave you the money to enter your local beauty pageant."

"It was the least he could have done after joining with the other kids and mocking me"—she chortled—"until he found me in the school cloak closet and fell in love with me."

"And after you won the pageant and Stu Silverman discovered you while he was passing through Pennsylvania, the photographer wanted blackmail money. As you told me, Stu paid the photographer off in exchange for the negatives."

"Which Stu held over my head after *On My Own* was a hit and I wanted to move on to a younger agent with more clout in Hollywood."

You only get one take, Jana. "How did you make the light screen fall?"

Christa smiled. "Everyone was focused on your scene. Nobody noticed when my foot knocked into the lighting screen."

"How did you know Stu would save you?"

"Stu was standing next to me. I was confident he would do anything to protect his star client."

"How did you know about hemlock and oleander?"

"I told you. I grew vegetables and herbs back home."

"It must have been difficult for you to sneak the herbs into your food without anyone noticing."

"As you remember, there was pandemonium when five minutes was called at the end of the lunch break. It was easy for me to slip the herbs from my purse into my plate, lay the plate on the end table, and pick up Stu's plate, leaving him to think my plate was his."

"And me to suspect that *you* were the target of the murderer—while you got rid of the elderly agent you saw as an albatross." Jana took a step closer to Christa. "And that left Nick as your next victim—to pay him back for not rescuing you years ago, and for trying to ride on your coattails now."

Christa laughed. "As an actress, you have to appreciate the sheer theatrics of me pushing Uncle Nick then falling into Andrew's unsuspecting arms, claiming I had been pushed."

"And for extra assurance that nobody would suspect you, this closet became your next stage. It kept haunting me that a razor blade was missing from its pack in the cabinet drawer."

"I had to find the blade to cut my leg—to appear as if I'd been attacked."

"Then you placed the bloody blade inside the rubber gloves you had also taken, and hid them in one of the legs of the screen."

"And like little Margaret in your movie, which

gave me the idea by the way, I lay on the floor and held my breath until I blacked out."

"Causing all of us to think you were the victim."

Christa smiled like the Cheshire Cat. "Leaving my greatest feat for scene five—your benefit."

"Where you killed the man who loved you."

Christa sighed. "Andrew loved me...in his way. But as you saw, he cheated on me in the guise of wanting to bring women to the Lord. Not to mention Andrew was manipulative and domineering. He wanted me to turn down Madame Curie to play a time traveling stewardess! That was the last straw."

Jana tented her fingers. "I wondered why you were wearing a cape on such a warm evening. My guess is you hid the knife in your purse. As you mentioned, you and Andrew cuddled throughout the evening. You rested your cape on the back of your chair. When you asked Andrew to switch seats with you, I assume you moved the knife from your purse to underneath the tablecloth to inside your cape, and then you stabbed him."

"The perfect ending to the perfect dinner: not being forced into giving birth to Andrew Jr." Christa groaned. "Could you imagine being nine months out of commission? And even worse, unleashing another whining Andrew on the world?"

"Then you pulled out the knife so no one would suspect your fingerprints being on it. And you mentioned Andrew was in your chair, so again everyone would suspect you were the target of the murderer. You gave quite a performance as the shocked and grieving widow."

"I know my craft," Christa replied proudly.

"Which will come in handy since with Andrew gone you inherit Nevgere Productions, and you are free to make your own career choices. I always thought Nevgere Productions was an odd name for a production company. Until I realized Nevgere is an anagram for 'revenge.'"

"And you figured it all out by remembering the plot of *School Spy*. I should have thought of that." Christa opened the bottle of pills. "What a shame that a woman with such a great mind has to leave us now. I really meant what I said about wanting to be your friend, Jana—if circumstances were different." Christa took a small bottle of water out of her purse. "It might have been easier if your test results weren't so good. But, as they say, God works in mysterious ways. Say a prayer that you go to Heaven."

"Odd that murder doesn't go against your religious beliefs, Christa."

"As you said, the Bible stories are for inspiration, not law. By the way, they are packed with violence and murder." Christa offered Jana the pill bottle and water. "Drink up."

"That's not going to happen, Christa."

"Yes, it is. After you left your house, I went there by taxi and told Missy you asked me to bring B.J. to you here."

Jana's heart skipped a beat. "Where is he?"

"Locked inside my hotel room. He's safe. For now."

B.J.!

But if you don't take every one of these pills, B.J. will meet the same fate as Stu, Uncle Nick, and Andrew." She rose and pushed the pills in Jana's face.

"Enjoy."

Using a move from *The Cutest Scientist*, Jana clasped her hands together and raised them upward, knocking the bottle out of Christa's hands. Rage filled Christa's face as she dove on top of Jana. Reminiscent of a scene from *Jungle Girl*, Jana pulled the back of Christa's hair until Christa screamed then Jana kneed her in the stomach. The door opened, and three police officers hurried inside. One handcuffed Christa, the second reached for the tape recorder, and the third grabbed Christa's arm and led her to the doorway.

"I'm on medication for a nervous breakdown due to my husband's death." Christa cried out, "I'm not responsible for what I'm saying. It's temporary insanity." She looked toward Jana. "She baited me!"

Jana smiled at Christa. "You've given your last performance, Christa."

"I want my Andrew! I want my husband!"

Once Christa and the officers were gone, Jana grabbed Clownie, hurried out of the room, and said to Detective Rivera and Bove in the hallway, "We have to get B.J.!"

Rivera replied, "When I received word that Mrs. Bianca left the hospital, I had one of my officers follow her. He found B.J. and brought him home safely. Your nanny is watching him."

"Thank God."

Bove said, "Rivera called me right after you called him."

Jana glared at them. "It took you long enough to come inside."

Rivera explained, "I wanted to make sure we had Mrs. Bianca's full confession on tape." He scratched the back of his head unleashing a whirlwind of white. "Thanks to you, Mrs. Otley, we do."

"Jana Lane saves the day again." Bove wrapped his arm around her. "Come on, *Girl Detective*, let's get you home."

Epilogue

1986

Jana Lane Otley wore a peach hostess dress and peach mascara with her hair in layers around her face. She closed the sky-blue curtains over the French doors in her cathedral-ceilinged great room. Glancing over at the bookcase next to the fireplace, she winked at the Emmy Award statue for Best Actress in a Dramatic Television Show, and Humanitarian Award plaque for her Jana Lane AIDS & Breast Cancer Foundation.

She smiled as her guests helped themselves to drinks and hot and cold gourmet snacks at the bar then sat on sofas, loveseats, and easy chairs around the room.

Checking her watch, Jana turned on the television set. The news announcer reported, "The investigation continues of President Reagan, Vice President Bush, and fellow Republicans McFarlane, Poindexter, Weinberger, and North for allegedly breaking Congress' Boland Amendment, by allegedly selling arms to Iran, allegedly endangering the lives of US hostages there, and allegedly being unable to account for the money made in the sales."

I've never heard the term 'allegedly' so many times in one sentence.

Bove rose from a loveseat and held his glass

toward the woman sitting next to him. "To the woman who has just agreed to be my wife—Cindi Vizard." Cindi blushed as the crowd applauded.

I hope this relationship lasts for you, Bove. Sitting on a sofa across from them, Jana said, "Congratulations, Bove. And good luck, Cindi."

As the crowd chuckled, Jana noticed Simon and Cornelius, Jackson and Adam, Hyo and Alaster, and Aisha and Siobhan each share a surreptitious glance. *Your day will come, chums.*

Cindi leaned over and whispered in Jana's ear, "The men who were after me are in prison on charges of theft." She patted Bove's knee. "Thanks to my fiancé."

Bove smiled proudly. "And I caught them without the help of Jana Lane."

"I have no doubt," Jana replied with a grin.

Bove rose again. "And congratulations to you, Jana Lane Otley, celebrated sleuth and everyone's best friend on screen and off."

Everyone cheered.

Simon waved his chartreuse scarf and shouted, "Speech! Speech!"

The group joined Simon.

Bove sat and Jana rose. "Thank you. But we have *all* worked hard this year on *The Detective's Wife*. So I would like to thank *you* regular co-stars on *The Detective's Wife* who have become my friends."

Bove, Cindi, Hyo, Alaster, Aisha, and Sibohan glowed like lanterns.

Jana raised her glass, "And I would also like to thank my amazing agent and his equally amazing partner."

Simon stood and bowed and Cornelius sat him back down.

"And my best friend Jackson and his best partner Adam whom I see far too infrequently."

Jackson and Adam blew kisses at her.

"To my terrific son's terrific nanny, Missy, and her fiancé, Officer Jason Franklin."

Missy and Jason shared a kiss.

"To Detective Rivera and his ever patient wife Consuela."

Mrs. Rivera used her husband's handkerchief to wipe a layer of his dandruff off the end table.

"To our adorable children upstairs, Devon, Ed, B.J. and their cousins Tyler and Topher who are no doubt all wide awake ready to cheer on B.J. in tonight's episode." Finally, Jana turned to Brian sitting next to her, and tears filled her eyes. "And to my real life partner in crime, my soulmate, and the love of my life. Brian, you are my past, present, and future." Brian stood, took her in his arms, and they shared a long, deep kiss.

As everyone cheered, the television announcer said, "And now it's time for the number one show on television, *The Detective's Wife*."

Jana sat next to Brian, rested in his strong arms, and looked around the room at her extended family. *There really is no place like home.*

Thank you for purchasing
this publication of The Wild Rose Press, Inc.

If you enjoyed the story, we would appreciate your
letting others know by leaving a review.

For other wonderful stories,
please visit our on-line bookstore at
www.thewildrosepress.com.

For questions or more information
contact us at
info@thewildrosepress.com.

The Wild Rose Press, Inc.
www.thewildrosepress.com

Stay current with The Wild Rose Press, Inc.

Like us on Facebook

https://www.facebook.com/TheWildRosePress

And Follow us on Twitter
https://twitter.com/WildRosePress